Baker's DOZEN

Dear Bill & Karon,
   Nancy & I pray for
God's blessing on you
and your family.
   Colin

Baker's DOZEN

CALVIN KENNETH NIX SR.

iUniverse, Inc.
Bloomington

Baker's Dozen

This is a work of fiction. All of the characters, names, incidents, organizations, and dialogue in this novel are either the products of the author's imagination or are used fictitiously.

iUniverse books may be ordered through booksellers or by contacting:

iUniverse
1663 Liberty Drive
Bloomington, IN 47403
www.iuniverse.com
1-800-Authors (1-800-288-4677)

Because of the dynamic nature of the Internet, any web addresses or links contained in this book may have changed since publication and may no longer be valid. The views expressed in this work are solely those of the author and do not necessarily reflect the views of the publisher, and the publisher hereby disclaims any responsibility for them.

Any people depicted in stock imagery provided by Thinkstock are models, and such images are being used for illustrative purposes only.
Certain stock imagery © Thinkstock.

ISBN: 978-1-4759-2520-3 (sc)
ISBN: 978-1-4759-2522-7 (hc)
ISBN: 978-1-4759-2521-0 (ebk)

Printed in the United States of America

iUniverse rev. date: 05/24/2012

This book is dedicated to the memory of my loving wife, Dochia, who for 61 years walked with me through this life with all its joys and sorrows. I have the comfort of knowing that Jesus has promised that one day we will be together again and we will walk hand in hand with Him forever. "Whosoever believeth in Him should not perish but have eternal life." John 3:15.

Dochia is greatly missed by me and our four children, Ken, Pam, Alan, and Allison, and a host of grandchildren and great-grandchildren.

ACKNOWLEDGEMENTS

The book would not have been possible without the help of my family. I thank each one of you.

My daughter, Pam typed the beginnings of the book and placed them on a disc. Ken, my eldest son, and his partner, Bev were a great help in preparing the book for editing. Thanks to my dear friend, Judy Nelson, who worked tirelessly typing, typing, and typing some more in order to ready the book for proof reading. Thank you to my son Alan who proofread the book and steered me in the direction of publication. I was cheered on by my youngest daughter, Allison, who supported me. My beautiful granddaughter, Lauren, took on the task of correcting and editing the final copy of the book. I thank each of you for your help, love and support.

ONE

It was 8:00pm on a Thursday evening when the 777 left the airport at Lucerne, Switzerland, with a destination of New York City. The 777 has always fascinated me as it was the first plane to be completely designed by a computer. Some contend that computers are smarter than humans, so it should be a good, safe flight. After working long, stressful hours at my latest assignment, my mind was full of unrest and excitement knowing there was another dangerous assignment awaiting me. As I drifted off to sleep, I wondered what adventure awaited the Bakers Dozen. Our team closed a difficult case that had been causing us trouble for over six months.

I should take a moment to digress and brief you on my occupation. My name is Jim Thompson, and I am an active special agent for the D.I.A., also known as the Department of Interior Action which fights crime on a worldwide level. I report directly to my boss, Admiral Alton Baker, and to the President of the United States. I am the type of Agent that gets commissioned for top secret missions and investigations. Our assignments are so classified that most of the time we do not notify the local authorities of our presence or interest in their local affairs.

Special Agent Odell Small and I met with Admiral Baker, and were given the orders to fly to Switzerland to investigate three U.S. Air Force planes that had come up missing. It took over six months for the government to determine that equipment and planes were missing! Luckily the crooks were sloppy and over anxious. It was a very simple task to follow their money trail to find out they had sold the planes and equipment for 87 million dollars.

We were able to recover some of the money and put the three crooks in jail.

Contrary to the popular belief that the government "wasted" money, D.I.A. agents do not get to fly first class. On just about every flight, I have somehow managed to get a talkative seat companion wanting to swap life histories or share findings from aimless Google searches on their laptops. I have even had parts of meals spilled on my lap a few times. I wish Congress would pass a law requiring all D.I.A. agents to travel first class. Until then, I must endure these long coach trips to and from assignment locations.

New York. I arrived on schedule and the April weather was phenomenal. Just the idea of being there created excitement as I remembered the good times spent there throughout the years. I have spent much of my time in the Big Apple receiving new assignments from the meetings held by the D.I.A., and have tried to enjoy as much as the city has to offer. I have seen many outstanding Broadway shows and have had many wonderful dining experiences.

Having to get through Customs has always been the most unpleasant aspect of arriving in the U.S. I often have been asked by family and friends how I am able to transport weapons in and out of the country without being harassed by Customs. D.I.A. agents have a special clearance that allows us to carry any type of weapon aboard any commercial plane or onto any military base. We always establish with authorities ahead of time when we are to take flight and show our badges upon arrival before we reveal our weapons. Sometimes custom agents don't receive the advance notice that we are arriving and consume a lot of our time questioning us about the weapons, and verifying our badges.

After finally clearing Customs, I took a cab to the New York Hilton, where all agents are to stay when in town. It seems that most New York Cabbies have the desire to either be a great orator or a race car driver; I was unfortunate enough to get one that had ambitions to be both. He had knowledge and opinions about everything. During the trip he enlightened me as to why all the taxi cabs rattled; it seemed that it was discovered several years ago that tires on the cabs would last longer if you increased the air pressure to 70 pounds. If passengers were irritated by the rattle, it was of no concern because more than likely the cabbie wouldn't have any certain passenger in his cab more than once. So, they aired the tires and the rattles came. Halfway towards our designation, I offered my driver a cough drop so he'd put a cork in it, but he refused. I think he got the message about his non-stop talking.

As I checked into the hotel, the clerk told me there was a piece of mail waiting for me at the postal office located within the hotel's lobby. The P.O. Box there was paid for by Admiral Baker to relay messages to the agents. As expected, there was a message that read as follows: "DFW Monday, April 15th, 11:00 a.m., Baker."

Many years ago the U.S. government designed, built, and leased certain buildings located near airports in most major U.S. cities to reliable companies. These buildings were designed to look as if they only had 12 floors, but in reality, they contained 13 floors. One half of each of the buildings' thirteenth floor was occupied by the D.I.A. The instructions in the message told me to proceed to DFW airport in Dallas, TX, and report to the thirteenth floor of the D.I.A. building located in Irving, Texas at 11A.M. the following day.

Irving is located in proximity to Arlington where "The Ballpark," home of the Texas Rangers is located. Arlington is also my home; I was able to spend some much needed time with the family. My wife, Helen, a flight attendant, was on a three day turnaround from DFW to London, and our kids, Ginger and Bill, were home from school, so I got tickets to the Ranger baseball game. I had not seen my family in a couple of months. We had a great time and ate way too many hot dogs and peanuts. We got to see Raphael Palmeiro hit home run number 500 and aid the Rangers to a victory. It was the perfect evening spent with my family before I received the assignment the next day.

Monday, April 15th. The scheduled meeting time was 11:00am, which gave me plenty of time for breakfast and just enough time to place a phone call to an old friend and Navy associate, W.J. Loggins. I had not talked with him in over a year. It was good to catch up with him and hear all about his family. Before we knew it, it was time for the meeting. So, we said goodbye and agreed to meet with our families real soon. As usual, I was fifteen minutes early for the scheduled meeting.

Several other agents were arriving about the time I checked in. Agent Small was one of early ones. He was six foot tall, well-built and had a neatly kept beard. He always chewed gum, which always played on my nerves. We worked together on several jobs in the past and I was not surprised to see him at this meeting.

We agents were visiting and renewing friendships when Admiral Baker came into the meeting room. We all call him "Admiral" because he was transferred to the D.I.A. from the Navy.

He began the meeting by telling us the President of the United States wanted to employ the D.I.A. to put a stop to some of the worst criminal activity on American soil. Organized crime had pushed drugs, prostitution, and murder to an all-time high. This was going to be a monumental task.

Agent Small and I were assigned to help prevent the selling and smuggling of illegal drugs. Rose Hope and Betsy Jones were assigned to aide us.

The President said, "Organized crime happens more often in states with smaller populations such as Louisiana, Arkansas and Texas. Unfortunately, murder has often accompanied the organized crime."

Admiral Baker told us that he had asked for twenty agents and had only received thirteen for this operation.

When we start on a new sting we always use code names for the operation. One of the agents, Jack Hallmark, said "when he was young there was a bakery near their house and when they bought a dozen donuts the baker would always give thirteen, which he called a baker's dozen. Therefore, we should be called the "Baker's Dozen." Of course Admiral Baker liked the code name.

Agents Odell Small, Rose Hope and Betsy Jones and I took our briefing kit to a far corner of the room to see what we were going to contend with. We would be looking into insurance fraud that might be tied to murder. The rest of the agents were assigned other projects.

TWO

Before starting this project we did the usual preparation that we do for all cases. We first established what we referred to as a "dummy" office in the insurance district of Hartford, Connecticut. Basically it was an office space that we could work our operations out of, but that looked like an insurance office. The name of our cover insurance company was "Alton Insurance." Next, we set up a dummy apartment in Windsorlocks, Connecticut just a short commute to Hartford. We installed four separate telephones at the apartment. The local telephone company answering service was used for messages. We set up a post office box, which would be checked daily by one of our local agents. We were given fake driver licenses, social security numbers, and "Alton Insurance" name badges. For all the general public knew, were official insurance fraud investigators.

The state of Connecticut had seven D.I.A. agents. The agents visited our dummy office and thought it had everything necessary to be a good central location for the seven of them. After reviewing the file, we decided to see how many insurance policies had been issued in the last five years for amounts of two million dollars or more in this four state area.

The first part of any investigation was typically rather slow, dull, and tedious, but it must be completed in order to narrow down the vast number of insurance where fraud was suspected. As a starting point, we decided to contact six of the largest insurance companies in the U.S. to get a list of all the policies received for over two million dollars in the last five years. Also, we needed a list of the policies that had death claims.

It took the four of us over two months of calls, letters, meetings and arm twisting to finalize this.

We successfully obtained all the lists we needed, complete with lists of policy holders. It appeared that most of the life insurance policies that fit the criteria, 377 to be exact, were taken out in Louisiana, Oklahoma, and Texas.

When a death claim was involved with the collection of an insurance policy, the insurance companies typically issued an initial policy, in our 377 cases that policy was for 2 million dollars in each count. Upon the results from an autopsy, the insurance companies paid out a second policy of the same amount as the first one. In order to narrow the scope of our investigation, we decided to put the cases in which the second policy was collected on hold. This left 174 cases left to be investigated first.

We decided to check our list of death claims against these, since not all 174 cases involved death claims, some involved houses burning down, car wrecks, etc. Of these 174 that just accepted the original policy of two million dollars, only five had death claims.

One of the five policies had been issued for the death of a successful female athlete. Her husband was suspected of her murder and was awaiting trial. Payment had been suspended until the conclusion of the trial. We decided to eliminate this case.

We then began analyzing the remaining four: one was in Louisiana, the second in Oklahoma, and the last two were in Texas.

The Louisiana case was assigned to Agent Jones; Small and Hope each took one of the Texas cases; I took the Oklahoma case.

In order to identify the cases involved in this investigation, we named the investigation "Henry" and gave each case a number: "Henry #1" was the first case, then there's "Henry #2" and so forth. The information gathered in each case was entered into the computer, and was also kept on paper in a file. The main thing we were investigating in these cases was to see if any foul play was suspected. Did the beneficiary stand to gain too much if the subject was to die?

Henry #1: Agent Jones' case in Louisiana. The policy holder's name was David Richards, the owner of a seafood restaurant in New Orleans. While in a meeting with city officials and zoning experts for the planning of a second restaurant, he suddenly collapsed and was rushed to a local emergency room where he died an hour and a half later. The doctor's report on the death certificate stated that it was a heart attack. His wife and personal physician both stated his blood pressure was elevated and out of control. Conclusion: fatal heart attack, no foul play suspected.

Henry #2: Agent Hope's Texas case. The subject was male, 36 years old and had been a stock broker for seven years. He lived in San Antonio, and was driving back from a training session in Corpus Christi with a fellow broker when tragedy struck: a bridge over a canal collapsed when one of its supports was hit by an out of control loaded barge. In total, nine people were killed. This case was listed as an accident; foul play was ruled out.

Henry #3: Agent Small checked on the second case in Texas. The subject was a 57 year old rancher who had been farming and raising cattle in west Texas all of his working life. The land he was working had been in his family for many years. In that part of the country, land prices fluctuated depending on the success of drilling on the land in search for water. Undrilled land prices were moderate, whereas land where water was found was priced ridiculously high. If a land was drilled and a dry well was found, the price of the land was dropped below that of undrilled land. As it so happened, the subject had found water wells on his land, and was using the water to irrigate his farm land. One day, he was struck by lightning while he and two Hispanic workers were herding some cattle during a thunder storm. The medics arrived as soon as weather conditions cleared enough for them to make safe passage to the ranch. Conclusion: accidental death by strikc of lightcning during a thunder storm.

Henry #4: My case in the southeast part of Oklahoma. The subject was a 64 year old man that evidently died from choking on a chicken bone, as indicated on his death certificate. His death occurred seven years after the policy was taken out.

To begin my investigation of this claim, I decided to press the local barber for information regarding the deceased. In a small town such as Alderson, there is only one barber in town, and the likelihood of him knowing the deceased was great. Plus, I really needed a haircut.

Without hesitation the barber told me he had known the subject for many years.

"What can you tell me about the deceased?" I asked him.

"He was a great guy!" The barber began. "We grew up here together. After high school he moved away for college, met his first wife, had two sons, and moved to the west coast."

"Did you say 'first wife?'"

The barber nodded his head. "After living out west for a while, he and his wife got a divorce. No one really knows why. Once the divorce was finalized, he moved back here and hooked back up with his high school sweetheart. They married two years later."

"Do you know anything about this second wife?"

"She is a sweet gal. Still lives at their place up on the hill outside of town. He was her second husband; her first died four years ago."

"How would you describe the relationship between her and your friend?"

"They were like love birds, totally inseparable. They were still married when he passed away."

I thanked the barber for his time, paid him for the trim, and decided to talk to the subject's widow next.

Outside of the barber shop was an old phone booth with an outdated phone book. Luckily, the phone book contained the listing for the widow. I placed a quick call to her, explained that I represented the insurance company and had been sent to follow-up with her to confirm the insurance money was received, and that she was satisfied. She seemed nice over the phone. Definitely sounded like a lifelong smoker. She took the bait, and we set an appointment to meet at her place at 3:00pm later that day.

I had no trouble finding the estate. After seeing the town, with its rundown buildings and out-of-service restaurants and gas stations, I was surprised to see such a stately and magnificent home. It was built in the ranch style form, and appeared to be about 4,000 square feet. Situated on several acres, it had a full-sized tennis court, swimming pool, and a mini golf course.

I rang the doorbell and was met by a beautiful blond woman in her mid-40s. She introduced herself as the subject's widow, and invited me in for coffee.

She explained that immediately after returning from the west coast, the subject began restoring and updating this home that he had lived in with his parents during his early years. It had been vacant for several years and needed a lot of work. After updating the house, he added the amenities outside.

I asked her "Were you aware of the reason your husband elected to take out a two million dollar insurance policy, showing you as the sole beneficiary?"

"During his lifetime, he had plenty of money," she began. "Most of the money came from a trust fund that his father set up when he was born. His father was a very successful oil wildcatter in Texas. The trust fund was set up so that in the event that my husband was to die, the money would pass along to his children. If there were no children, the money would go to a designated charity."

"So he placed you as the beneficiary because you would not receive any money if he died?"

"Once we were married, he had the policy changed to place me as the beneficiary so that I would be taken care of."

When I got back to the office in Irving, Agent Small had completed Henry #3 and was checking up on the cases where the second two million dollar policy had been accepted. Even though we had eliminated these cases originally, Agent Small had a feeling that foul play might have been involved in a few of the cases.

Seven death claims were made in the past five years against these policies. Agent Small had been able to obtain copies of the death certificates. Four showed the cause of death to be accidents or natural causes; three showed the cause of death to be undetermined.

The rest of the team assembled in Irving. Once everyone was up to speed on the individual findings, we contacted Admiral Baker. After summing up the five cases that were investigated where only the first policy was collected on, Agent Small discussed the three larger cases that he found where the second policy was accepted. Admiral Baker instructed us to look into these cases next. However, we were all in need of a small break. Admiral Baker granted us each a week for a vacation and time with our families. We all shook hands and parted ways.

Several years ago, the family and I were on driving home from the Thompson family reunion held at Ft. Gibson Lodge in northeast Oklahoma when we found a very unique cabin close to Ten Killer Lake in Oklahoma. The scenery around the lodge was breathtaking, and we decided to spend a few days there. Ginger and Bill had a blast going horseback riding, fishing and biking. The lodge also had a recreation center with a gym, video arcade, and movie theater.

We have gone there every summer since then, and to no surprise I took my week off to take the family back there. While working on these long assignments, it is vitally important to me to spend time with my family.

THREE

Feeling refreshed from our vacation time, we all felt full of energy and zest. We were ready to start the next phase of the investigation. Now we were to look into the three cases where the second policy was collected, where the cause of death was uncertain.

The three subjects were all business owners:, subject # one had three barbecue restaurant locations, subject #2 had two automatic car washes, and the third subject had a large auto junk yard. We thought it best if two agents would start on the legwork of the first case and the other two agents would do preliminary investigation on the other two cases

Agent Hope, the veteran among our group, was elected to investigate the first case. I, being the so called rookie because I had the least number of years of service in the D.I.A., and was assigned to go with her. She pitched the idea that I was to act like I was a new insurance investigator in training, and our purpose in investigating the case was to train me how to investigate a fraudulent claim. Clever. I think she really wanted to keep me quiet and allow herself the opportunity to do all the talking during the investigation.

Henry #5: The subject was owner of a barbeque restaurant at three different locations at various exit ramps along I-30 in Texas. After checking in to our hotel, Agent Hope thought that we should begin by contacting the subject's widow. She placed the call and scheduled the meeting at the widow's home at 3:30pm.

13

We arrived at the widow's house promptly at 3:20pm. It was beautiful, and clearly expensive, situated on about eight or ten acres, with a half mile long driveway lined with pine trees. There was a brick fence across the front of the home, which allowed for moderate privacy and yet was highly stylish. There appeared to be a large warehouse of some sort towards the back of the property.

The widow greeted us at the door with fresh coffee and oatmeal raisin cookies. We graciously accepted, and she led the way to her formal sitting room located in the front room to the right of the expansive entry hall.

Agent Hope explained to the widow that I was a newly employed with the insurance agency and it was her job to train me.

"Please tell us a little bit about your late husband?" Hope began. "What did he do for a living?"

"He was a very kind, caring man. Very skilled with his hands; he was a machinist, and worked for a tool and die maker company. On his spare time, he restored old cars."

"Sounds like a hardworking man. How long have you been living in this house?"

"We bought this land after we had been married for about two years. It was our dream property. We drove by the acreage almost on a weekly basis for a whole year before we saw a for sale sign put up. We acted immediately. First my husband built the large building in the back of the property. That's where he would work on the cars. Throughout the years, when he would take on a different kind of car, he would need new equipment to help with the restoration. He had quite a collection of gadgets, thus the need for the large shed. Later, he built the house based on a picture in a magazine that I loved."

"What would he do with the cars once he completed them?"

The widow smiled. "Each time he finished a car some of his friends would try to buy it. He always became too attached and would refuse to sell. He had to add space to the warehouse in order to house all the cars. I still have all of them."

Agent Hope made note of this on her pad of paper. "Did your husband have any other interests?"

"He loved to cook barbeque and had a passion for it like no one I've ever met. It was the best barbeque in these parts. The secret was his sauce. Our friends were always requesting him to make some for them, and he started taking orders. Then, our friends encouraged him to open a small restaurant so he could sell ribs. He finally agreed and found a little space in town. He would hook up his smokers to the back of the building and served ribs and brisket Fridays and Saturdays. Business thrived and he was able to hire workers and go full time."

The widow paused to refresh our coffee. "Business continued to flourish, and we soon opened the barbeque restaurants at two more locations. Of course he quit his job as a machinist, but he still restored cars in his spare time. After the third restaurant was opened, we decided to build the home that you are in now. Even though the land was paid for, we had to get a loan to build the house. This was a loan for $925,000. The bank gladly loaned that amount since the business was doing great. About a year after we completed the construction of our home, a piece of property became available that my husband had been wanting. He wanted to buy it so he could build a small chain of lease spaces. He wanted to open the fourth restaurant in one of the spaces and contract the other spaces to other businesses for additional profit."

"You said he wanted to buy it. Was he able to?" I asked the widow.

"We were unable to obtain a loan for the property since we had just taken out the large loan for our house. However, the bank manager did refer my husband to an individual who was new in town and had recently opened a very large account at the bank. This individual had told the manager that he had a privately funded business that loaned money to companies that were successful, but in need of money above sound business practices. They wanted payments of just interest for a ten year period, after which the whole note would be due and payable. In exchange for a lenient payment plan, they wanted 10 percent of the stock of the company they helped to fund, and a two million key man policy payable to the corporation. If the president of the company were to die before the ten years interest period expired, the loaning individual would pay off the note and give some funding to the company to hire a new president. Another two million dollar policy would be taken out on the life of the president with the company as beneficiary. These funds would be used to buy his portion of the stock from his widow. Necessary agreements would have to be signed to assure that this would transpire."

"Sounds almost too good to be true," finally I was able to get a word in.

"Yes, it sounded pretty good to my husband. However, up until that point we were the sole owners of the business, and this deal would mean that we would have to incorporate. After much discussion, my husband and I decided that we would take the deal. We gathered the information needed to contact the investor from the bank manager. Everything went according to plan. He got the loan. He only had to pay interest for a ten year period. Nothing of the money could be paid on the principal during that ten year period. Before long, the new restaurant was up and running. He had leased some of the adjacent spaces to other businesses. It appeared that things were working out as he had planned. He was still restoring old cars in his spare time and was getting a good collection of antique cars."

This time, Agent Hope refreshed our coffees, and I grabbed another cookie. "Was your husband in good health at the time of his death?"

"Honestly, I was worried that he was working too hard between all the restaurants and the restoration of cars.

"I kept after him to get a complete physical from our family doctor. Finally about two years after the deal on the new restaurant, he agreed to have a complete health check-up. The doctor said that he was in excellent health. Blood pressure, cholesterol, prostate and so forth checked out to be in good health. This is why his death was such a shock. He died a couple of weeks after his medical check-up."

"Can you tell us about your husband's last few days?" I asked.

"Well, he had a one o'clock meeting with some business associates on that Friday before his death. He came home from the meeting around 5:00 and seemed completely normal. Saturday morning we were getting our overnight bags together for a weekend trip to the lake with some friends. I went to check on him, and he looked at me with a blank expression, then fell over and died. That was 1:30pm. He never gave any indication that anything was wrong. The autopsy did not reveal anything. They said his heart just stopped pumping, but could not determine any reason for that. The medical examiner ruled out heart attack as a cause of death, as his heart was normal. There was also no sign of any dangerous foreign substance in the blood or in the stomach. The medical examiner wrote the cause of death to be 'heart stoppage' with the cause unknown."

"What do you think caused your husband's death?" I couldn't resist asking for her opinion.

With a baffled look, she simply replied, "I have no idea."

Agent Hope and I thanked her for her time and said we would get in touch with her if we found out anything at all. This case was really quite interesting. Something was definitely not right.

Our next course of action was to obtain all the medical reports pertaining to our subject, including the autopsy and the interviews from medical personnel involved with his case. It was already after five, and the medical examiner's office was closed. We retreated back to the hotel and ordered room service for dinner, so we could stay in the hotel room and sort out the details of what the widow had told us.

At 10:30am the following morning, after a delicious continental breakfast of toast, eggs, bacon and coffee, we made our way to the office of the M.E. It was a short drive and we found it with no difficulty.

Bottom line, there has to be some reason for death. People don't just drop dead. Hearts don't just stop without an apparent reason. Usually heart stoppage is related to lethal combinations of prescription medication, drugs, poor health, or heart attack. We needed to establish a cause of death for this subject, if for no other reason than to ease that poor widow's mind.

After greeting us, the medical examiner led us into a small conference room at the front of the building where the other medical personnel on the staff during the autopsy of our subject were seated around a conference table. We joined them at the table and grabbed a fresh cup of coffee they had set out for us.

"We are really glad that someone is looking into this case. We all sensed that there must have been some wrongdoing for this poor man's heart to stop. This was actually the third case in the past year where the victim's heart apparently stopped beating, for a reason undetermined. Immediately after this autopsy we contacted the Sheriff's office and the District Attorney's office to plea some sort of investigation to take place," said the M.E.

"Was an investigation carried out?" Agent Hope asked, while I jotted down notes on my legal pad.

The M.E. shook his head, "No one seemed to be interested in this case, or the two other cases before it."

One by one the other doctors seated around the table filled us in on the details of the other two cases, as well as the procedure conducted for the autopsy of our subject. They assured us they ran every test available and in each case came to the same conclusion that cause of the heart stoppage was unknown. There was no apparent damage to the heart.

Agent Hope felt that it would aid our investigation if we could contact the surviving family members of the other two individuals where cause of death had not been determined. The M.E. freely gave us the last known addresses of the two victims and any other information he thought would be helpful.

Henry #6: We contacted the victim's widow. To avoid suspicion, we changed our identification to that of employees of the Health Department and explained that we were investigating local deaths where there was no known cause of death determined. We told her we were trying to find the cause of death on a particular policy holder in which the description of his death was similar to that of her husband. Reluctantly she agreed to talk to us and we made an appointment to visit with her for the following afternoon.

We pulled up to the wife's residence at about noon that next day. Her home was located in a very nice, middle class area. She offered some fresh tea and finger sandwiches.

"Thank you for agreeing to meet with us on such a short notice," Agent Hope began. "We are sorry for your loss."

It had been only a few months since her husband had passed. The widow seemed to soften up at Hope's condolences.

"Were you aware of any medical condition that your husband had that might have caused his death?"

"Oh no, he was in excellent health. In fact, he had a complete check-up about six months ago. Everything looked great. The doctor said that he was just five pounds over the ideal weight for his age of 61 years old. He sustained from alcohol. He was just about the picture of good health."

She continued with his story and told us that he had two businesses that furnished bail bonds to people so that they could be released from jail. They had opened their second bond shop location just a few months ago.

"How was business going?"

"As far as I knew, business was pretty good. I tried not to get too involved in his business affairs." She paused to slice up some apple pie for dessert.

Following up on a hunch on the patterns derived from our preliminary investigations of the other claims, Agent Hope asked, "Did your husband go to any sort of meeting or gathering before he died?"

"Let me think . . . yes he did actually. A couple of weeks before he died, we received an offer to buy out the business. My husband did not want to, but agreed to meet with the people that placed the offer to hear them out. The meeting was at 2pm on a Friday. He died suddenly at 3:30pm the following day."

Taking on a sympathetic tone, I asked her if she could tell us about her husband's death.

"Sure." She started to tear up. "I walked outside to the backyard to check on him. He was supposed to be bathing the dog. When I walked outside, he was standing still. The dog was running around barking and acting crazy. Instantly I knew something was wrong. A few seconds later, he fell over and died. I called the ambulance, but he was already dead when they arrived."

Agent Hope reached over and held her hand to comfort her. After a few moments, we continued the conversation.

"Right after he died, I received an offer from the same people as before to buy the business. I was depressed, and overwhelmed with trying to do it on my own, so I talked it over with my banker and my C.P.A. They were old family friends and had my best interest at heart. They both agreed that it looked like a very fair offer. I accepted the offer and had my lawyer draft up a contract."

When we left the widow's house, our adrenaline was pumping. Several of the subjects we have investigated took part in some sort of business meeting within 24 hours of dropping dead. There has got to be something to this.

We talked with Agents Small and Jones about our progress. They were still in the Irving office catching up on paperwork of the investigation.

Henry #7: This was the second of the two cases the Sheriff referred us to. There wasn't any insurance claim involved in this one. The subject was the owner of a very large plant nursery and landscape company. He started the business twelve or thirteen years ago. Business was booming: the nursery was selling more trees and shrubs each year; the landscape company was also increasing annually.

I called the widow, with the identity of the Health Department employee. In the interest of saving time, I held this interview over the phone with her. Through conversation, I learned that the husband was in excellent health. Business was better than ever, and he had several trustworthy employees. He liked to be hands-on in the various landscape jobs, and would drive around from job site to job site lending a hand and "getting his dose of vitamin D" as he would say. She said that she and her husband were sitting on the patio one evening discussing the upcoming plans for the weekend and without any warning he fell over and died. I asked her if he had any meetings with old friends or business associates immediately prior to his death. Following the pattern we noticed in the previous cases, she confirmed that he did in fact have a meeting with some business people the afternoon before his death. He said that they were interested in buying the company. Immediately after his death, they contacted her to make the offer to buy the company again. After talking to her accountant, she agreed and negotiated a price that was acceptable for both parties. She was relieved to get rid of the company since she didn't know anything about how to run the business, and it reminded her too much of her late husband. When questioned what she thought of the findings of the autopsy report, she told me, "These things just happen sometimes."

I got off the phone with her and headed back to the Irving office. There was definitely something fishy going on. Two undeniable facts kept surfacing in each individual case: the cause of death was unknown and the deceased had been in a business meeting within 24 hours prior to death. Also, immediately after death, the widows were approached by business offers to purchase the husband's companies.

FOUR

When we returned to the office in Irving, we found that Agents Small and Jones had finished up the paperwork on their part of the investigation so far. This was good news for us because it allowed us time to type up our reports while they took the next case assignment.

Henry #8. The subject was owner of two automatic car wash locations. The second location opened about six months ago. He had been unable to secure a loan from the bank to purchase the property and to build a car wash and also construct on the property four rental revenue units. However, the banker referred the subject to a customer that was a private investor who makes business loans with conditions that include incorporating a business, giving 10% of ownership to the lender and a ten year note with interest only for ten years. The subject had taken two insurance policies in the amount of two million each. One of these would be payable to the subject's widow for all of the outstanding stock in the subject's name. The other two million would be a key man policy payable to the corporation to assist the transition to the new management.

In fact, everything was going great and the subject was thinking of getting a third location for a car wash. He had a meeting with the same business friends just that afternoon before he died. He was pretty excited about the possibility of the third location and was talking to his wife about it the next afternoon when he died. His widow said that she had questioned the doctors and medical examiners about the cause of death. They both assured her they had made every possible test, and could find no reason for his death. His heart seemed to be okay. But, it just stopped. Everything else was normal. No sign of poison or anything else to cause the heart to stop. Agents Small and Jones thanked her for discussing this subject with them. The interview went pretty fast so they decided they would go right on to the next insurance case.

Henry #9: The subject was the owner of a large junk yard. Agent Jones set up an appointment to speak with the widow about facts surrounding her husband's death, in order to seek an explanation for the cause of his death. She told them she was happy to have them come out, and that she has not been able to have any peace over her husband's passing because the cause had not been resolved.

The agents were taken by surprised when they approached her house the next day. First of all, this was a very fine neighborhood, many fine homes on large lots. The widow's house appeared to be the finest in the area. The house stood on about six or seven wooded acres. It had a three foot white stone fence that had columns three or four feet high about every twenty feet with wrought iron fencing between each column. The house itself could have easily been called a palace, with its enormous porch and marble front steps. It looked large enough for a family of ten or twelve and contained six-car garage. They were greeted at the door by a maid who showed them into the library. There they were introduced to the subject's widow and to their surprise, her attorney.

The attorney was the first to speak. "I am here simply as a safeguard to be certain that you are not here to scam Mrs. Smith". Ever since her husband died, she has been hounded by many people trying to cheat her out of her money. It's nothing personal against you; we just need to take precautions. May I take a look at your identification?"

They showed him their "Alton Insurance" badges and gave them the number to their supervisor. After placing the phone call and determining that they represented no threat, the conversation resumed. The call he place actually just went to another agent at the dummy office in Hartford, Connecticut.

Agent Jones explained that they were checking insurance claims where there had not been found any reason for the cause of death.

"Can you tell us anything about your husband's life during the last ten years? Anything you think might have been unusual or that may have seemed out of place?"

"I am so glad you are looking into this. I was so frustrated that the District Attorney thought it would be a waste of time to look into my husband's sudden death." She glanced at her attorney before continuing, "Before we met, my husband was hired by a very large and prosperous law firm. He was assigned to handle land condemnation cases, the kind where the government tried to get people to sell their land for government use. His fee was based on an hourly rate for routine work and increased greatly if he had to go to court to settle a case. There were also rates for legal assistants, secretaries, court document search clerks, and so forth. For everything there was a charge. Of course there was another arrangement if a client did not have the money to pay on this scale. Then they would take a case for one half of the gain over and above the original offer by the government agency.

"He worked at this for two years. He was being paid above what most young attorneys were receiving. Still, he was not happy with his profession. He thought that the world would be better off with fewer attorneys. He disagreed with his fellow lawyers that would sue anybody for anything at any time. This is when he decided to do something else for a living. He decided to make a deal to purchase a wrecking yard. He said that some called it a 'junk yard' but legally it was called a wrecking yard. He purchased one and proceeded to take over management. This was a good business but he wanted it to do much better. He started selling some of the older cars to a company that would come by with a car crusher and load them onto a truck and pay him a fee for old junk cars. After a year of this he decided to change the way business was being done. He had just been selling parts as needed. He decided to keep certain makes and year models to sell parts to retail customers. Others, he would remove certain parts; starter, generator, air conditioner compressors and so forth and sell them to rebuilders and then crush the remainder. This worked great."

"Were you already married to him when this was going on?" Agent Jones inquired.

"We actually met about that time and married several months later. We had been married about a year when we found the property that our house is built on."

"Do you mind if we ask you how you paid for the land and house? Did you take out a loan?"

"Luckily, no, we didn't have to take out a loan. He had received money from a trust fund while he was in law school. It was more than enough for expenses so he was able to set some money aside. I assumed the fund ran out when he finished law school. About three months before his death he indicated that something was concerning him financially, and that he had to make a few financial changes. He also took out a couple of life insurance policies. He told me that a group of investors had contacted him several times and were trying to pressure him to sell his business. He had become nervous about their inquiries."

"What kind of financial changes did he make?"

"First of all, he incorporated the business, 45% of stock to him, 45% to her, and 10% to a trustee. This is the same trustee that was in charge of the trust that gave him income when he was in school. When he revealed all of this to me I asked why he was doing this. He said he was nervous about the group was trying to buy his business. He revealed the trust provided him with income while he was in school. However he, although he was the only beneficiary, had not received any funds from that trust since completing law school. He told me the value of the trust was twenty-seven million dollars."

Agent Small looked puzzled by that piece of information. "If he had a trust fund of 27 million dollars, why did he also take out the life insurance policies? It seems to me that 27 million dollars would be plenty of an inheritance to take care of you and the business."

"He told me that he wanted to be sure I would be ok in the event of his death. The insurance money would be just a back-up to make sure I was ok. It totally freaked me out that he was talking about death all of a sudden."

She then told the agents that the life insurance was in the amount of four million: two million payable to the company to finance problems after his death and two million to be used to purchase the stock from her. This would still leave her with 45% that she would receive from her husband's will and the trustee would still get 10%.

"Also, he had designated that I would be the only recipient of the trust money. The afternoon before his death he told me that he had met with the group that had been trying to purchase his business and told them firmly he did not wish to sell and requested they not contact him anymore. He seemed relieved he had made that decision. About 5 p.m. the next afternoon is when he died."

The agents thanked her and her attorney for their time and all the information she provided them and promised if they came up with anything they would notify her.

When Agents Jones and Small returned to the office in Irving they revealed to Agent Hope and me their findings. We summarized the cases we had worked on up until this point and analyzed them by making a chart displaying all the important details of each of the Henry cases:

	#1	#2	#3	#4	#5	#6	#7	#8	#9
Insurance Claim?	Y	Y	Y	Y	Y	N	N	Y	Y
$2 Million Claim	Y	Y	Y	Y	N	N	N	N	N
>$2 Million Claim	N	N	N	N	Y	N	N	Y	Y
Companies Incorporated	N	N	N	N	Y	N	N	Y	Y
Unknown cause of death	N	N	N	N	Y	Y	Y	Y	Y
Foul play suggested?	N	N	N	N	Y	Y	Y	Y	Y

As a result of the chart, it appeared that Henry cases five, six, seven, eight and nine were the key cases of interest, where the foul play was suggested. In each of those cases, the cause of death was unknown. Except for number six and seven, each case involved two policies of two million dollars each.

What else did the chart reveal? The businesses in five, eight and nine were incorporated just before the death of the owners. Of these five cases, all of the business would most likely have received income in the form of cash money.

All of this taken into consideration, there was good indication that something suspicious happened within 24 hours prior to death of each subject. Could it have something to do with the meeting that each subject took part in the day before their death? Possibly.

We contacted Admiral Alton Baker to relay the information derived from the analysis of the cases. Without delay, he booked a flight and planned to meet with us on Monday at 2:00pm.

FIVE

Admiral Baker arrived at the Irving office at 2:00 p.m. Monday afternoon and instantly wanted updates on the investigation.

After looking at the chart and hearing what we had to say, Baker took a few seconds to process all of the information.

"Good job everyone. All of the information you have gathered seems to show without a doubt that these cases were related. Too many details are reoccurring among them. It does appear as a large operation of organized crime." Baker cleared his throat. "I think we need to broaden the scope, and see if there is more indication of criminal activity mirroring our cases happening nationwide. Let's start by teaming up with three other agents in Georgia, Oregon, and California."

I was the first to speak. "What preparatory steps need to be made prior to meeting these other agents?"

"First we will need to get 'Alton Insurance' ID badges made for them, this will take two to three days. They will need to be briefed on the investigation. Small, send over the computer reports to each agent. Here are their names and email addresses. Make sure to encrypt the information, and mark it as 'highly confidential.'" He passed over a piece of paper to Agent Small.

"We have already established commonality between the cases, and we know there is some sort of organized criminal activity going on here. What we need to focus our efforts on now is to identify if there is one common group of criminals behind these cases. Furthermore, we need to know what is causing these deaths. Sure looks like murder, but we need proof. Understood?"

After the meeting adjourned, we hurriedly wrapped up all of our paperwork and divvied out the assignments on which agent was going to which state. Agent Hope was to go to Oregon; Agent Small to Georgia. An hour later, a call came in from Agent Willie Ackin, the agent in Oregon. His call was transferred to Agent Hope.

"Hello agents. I received the computer reports you sent to me a couple of hours ago. I'm really anxious to get started! Is there anything I can do to help before you arrive in Oregon?" Willie asked Agent Hope.

Agent Hope paused for a moment to think. "Actually it would help us if you would contact local insurance companies and retrieve reports where claims were filed on cases where the cause of death was unknown."

"No problem, the reports will be gathered and waiting for your arrival. Have a safe flight. Oh! When should I expect your arrival?"

Agent Hope glanced at her flight itinerary. "I'll be there tomorrow, before noon." They hung up the call and resumed work.

Agent Hope arrived at the office in Oregon just before noon on Tuesday. Agent Ackin was waiting with information that was requested. Agent Hope briefed him on the commonalities of the previous cases, and pointed out the facts of interest relevant to our investigation.

"Ackin, the main thing we are looking for is if there was an insurance claim involved? If so, did the subject take out the second two million dollar claim? Also, was the company incorporated prior to the death of the deceased? Was the cause of death unknown? Lastly, and this one may not be apparent on paper, but did the deceased participate in a business meeting of any kind within 24 hours of his/her death? We have a strong intuition that something occurred at the meetings that the subjects took part in before their deaths!"

After pouring over the paperwork, Agents Hope and Ackin were able to narrow down the number of cases down to two possibilities, based on the criteria. However, Ackin pointed out that even though both cases showed the cause of death to be unknown, only one case had the insurance claim collected. Also, the company was not incorporated prior to the death of the owner. The other case did have a small insurance policy with the cause of death unknown; however the subject in this case had been in poor health for some time.

They decided to begin the legwork of their investigation with the first case where there wasn't an insurance claim. After giving the subject's widow the same cover story used before, Agent Hope was able to set up an appointment for the following morning at 10:30am at the widow's house.

The widow seemed to be elated they were investigating her husband's case. Agent Hope asked her if she would retell the events of the last two years that might be of interest to us, especially if her husband acquired new business associates, new friends or anything else she could think of.

She readily agreed. "I'm sorry I look like such a mess. I was absolutely shocked by my husband's death. I'm still grieving. He had always been in good health and called himself very healthy. In fact, he always referred to himself 'The healthy Italian.'"

She said that they had been married about twelve years. "The first five years he was a chef in small Italian restaurant. He really had a passion for cooking. He had dreams of opening his own restaurant, and in due time he found a location that would be ideal to make his dream a reality. Luckily, the price was reasonable.

"Soon after starting his own restaurant business was great. A lot of his customers from the small restaurant followed him over to his restaurant. Less than two years later he had the opportunity to buy an old warehouse that was in good condition. Of course, he had to do a lot of work in order to make it into a restaurant. But he did this without too much effort or expense. He had the best equipment in the kitchen but just plain tables and chairs. Business was good but he owed a good bit of money on the building and also to the bank for the improvements."

Agent Ackin took detailed notes. He jotted down the last bit about the second restaurant, and then asked, "Do you know when your husband took out the life insurance policies?"

"It was about a year ago. I know that he took out two policies for two million dollars each, payable to me. We had lengthy discussions about how the money should be spent in the case of his death, and we actually have all the details written on paper. The first policy was to be used to pay off any money owed by the restaurant and to assist in hiring new management. The second policy was to take care of my expenses, so that I could live relatively financially comfortable on my own. Even though we mapped out the details on paper, we didn't think that it would ever actually happen since he was in such great health. I still can't believe he is gone!"

"Did your husband by any chance receive any offers to buy his business before his death?" Agent Hope asked on a hunch.

"Why, yes he did. I believe it was a few months ago. An agent that represented a group of investors called him with an offer to buy the restaurant. My husband told him that we were not interested in selling the restaurant. Business was flourishing, why would we want to sell it?"

"Did your husband ever meet with the agent or any of his associates?"

"He did the day before he died. The agents kept bothering us, you know, calling and leaving voicemails, stopping by the restaurant and such. He finally caved in and met the agent and two of the investors at a local bar for a couple of drinks. The investors had already contracted up an offer, even though we never gave any inclination to selling it. My husband said he was furious when he saw the contract, and made it clear to them once more that he was absolutely not going to sell at this point in time. He requested that they refrain from contacting him."

"How would you describe your husband's behavior or feelings after the meeting adjourned?" asked Agent Ackin.

"He seemed relieved. He said that he felt he got the message across clear enough, and that he doubted he would be contacted by them again."

Agent Hope inquired, "How soon after he met with the agent and investors did your husband die?"

The widow raised her eyebrows in surprise by the question. "He died the next afternoon. We still do not know what caused his death."

"Have you heard from the agent since your husband's death?" Agent Hope asked.

"Shortly after his death, I would say about two months, the agent contacted me and made yet another offer to buy the restaurant. The amount he offered seemed to be fair and I already considered selling at that point. I had barely been out of bed during those two months, and was already feeling the pressure of taking on the business by myself. I had my accountant look over the contract and we decided to counter with a twenty-five percent raise in selling price. To our surprise, they agreed. We closed the deal last week. I feel that I did the right thing, but I'm sure my husband is rolling over in his grave at all of this."

Agent Hope and Willie thanked her and left.

"How do you think this case stacks up against the other ones you have dealt with?" Agent Ackin asked Hope.

"This business was never incorporated, whereas the main cases of interest from before were. It is the same in that the ownership changed right after the subject's death, and that the subject had died shortly after a meeting with potential buyers. The Medical Examiner was unable to determine a cause of death, and concluded that no foreign substance had entered his body, based on the death certificate we looked at prior to coming."

"Well I guess you are headed back to Irving now? I hope you enjoyed your stay in Oregon! Come back any time!"

"Thanks, Ackin. Have fun on your next assignment. Thanks for your help on this one!"

And with that Agent Hope headed back to Irving.

The next case we needed to investigate was in Georgia. Grady Sutton, the agent located there, had recently become available to assist us. I asked if he would retrieve lists of policies taken out for two million, with an addition of two million accepted, where there was also a death claim with the cause unknown. He said he would and would contact us as soon as he had the information.

The four of us agents, Hope, Johnson, Small and I, were at the office in Irving catching up on paperwork when we received word from Agent Sutton. He was able to locate one case that met the criteria for our search.

Agent Small said that he would join him in Georgia in two days and for Sutton to set up meetings with the Medical Examiner and the subject's widow for then. This case was assigned Henry #11.

Henry #11: The subject was the owner of a very large peach orchard. There were a lot of these in Georgia, but this one was about three hundred acres and well-manicured. It looked like a beautiful park but had to require a great amount of working order to make it look so great.

Grady had made an appointment with subject's widow for two p.m. on the afternoon of Agent Small's arrival. So, when Agent Small got to the office he and Grady proceeded to the appointment.

The subject's widow seemed to be grateful that they had come. Her mother and father had flown in from their home in Wyoming to visit her for a few days. Although Grady had previously explained to the widow why they were there, he repeated the reason again for the benefit of her parents.

"It's such a shame what happened to our son-in-law," began the dad. "We have not been at ease with the results from the autopsy. People do not just drop dead for any unknown reason."

"My husband was only 47 and was in very good health."

Agent Small nodded his head in understanding. "I know this might seem like a jump in topics, but what can you tell us about your husband's business relations over the past ten years? Has there been anything that you can recall being out of the ordinary or suspicious?"

"Well we have had the orchard for seventeen years. We furnish peaches to many supermarkets. As you can see, we live on the orchard as well, so it's easy to keep track of how the peaches are doing, and we can give undivided attention to them. A couple of years ago my husband built a shed close to the road, the one that was on your left when you drove in, where we would sell peaches to local residents. Three years ago the state condemned three and one half acres on the back side of the orchard and built a new highway. We were devastated at first from the loss of land, but soon saw the potential. My husband constructed a retail outlet on our property right off the new highway to sell peaches. We hired a local company to process our peaches into jars with our label. They also made jelly and purchased other food items and had labels placed on them. Business was much better than he had expected."

"Did your husband ever receive any offers to buy the orchard?" asked agent Small.

"Last year an agent contacted him and said that he had a group of investors who wanted to purchase his business. He told the agent that he was not interested in selling. About three or four months before his death he was contacted again. He repeated the no sale statement. Later the agent contacted him and said that he realized that the business was not for sale but asked if he would just meet with him and an investor just to let the investor know that he had been trying to represent them and make contact with the owner."

"Did they ever meet in person?"

"They did meet the afternoon before my husband's death. After that meeting he had seemed to be in good spirits. He said that he thought that they now understood that he was not going to sell."

"Have you heard from them since your husband's death?"

The widow began, "yes they have contacted me a couple of times. I told them that I appreciated the offer; it was more than the business was worth, but I was not interested in selling. I then asked that they not contact me again. They respected my wish and I have not heard from them again."

She and her parents expressed their thanks to Agents Small and Grady and asked to be notified if anything positive came from their investigation.

While on the flight back, Agents Small and Grady typed up a report on what they had learned from this investigation. Once this was completed and the flight landed, Agent Small returned to the office in Irving while Agent Grady was given a new assignment.

In Irving, Small discussed the findings with Agents Jones, Hope and I. There was yet one more case in California that needed to be investigated. After catching all the agents up to speed, we decided to contact Admiral Baker for further guidance. We needed a plan. It was late in the day, so we agreed to think about the problem this weekend and first thing Monday we would update the chart and summarize the information gathered thus far.

Well rested on Monday morning, we were all pretty excited to delve back into the case. Everyone seemed refreshed except for Agent Hope who said she had trouble sleeping because her mind was wrapped around the investigation. Agent Small said that it looked to him as if there was Mafia connected due to the fact that all of the cases seemed to have a lot in common even though they were in different parts of the country.

I agreed with Small's assumption.

We listed what we knew. The Henry cases 5-11 all had meetings 24 hours before death. Some were incorporated and had new owners. All had part of the income in the form of cash. We all thought this could be a way of organized crime to launder a great deal of cash. If this was true, how was it done? The circumstances that surrounded these deaths, all within 24 hours of a meeting with potential buyers, shed a very suspicious sense on the investigation.

Now, as to information we still lacked: were the new owners connected to each other; and did business profits change when the new owner took control?

Our next course of action was to see a list of all officers, stock holders, directors, employees and anyone with a working contract to see if there are any overlapping players that might indicate the cases were connected.

Admiral Baker said he would be in our office about 11:00 a.m. Thursday morning and that he would have a representative from the IRS with him. He wanted us to be prepared to brief the IRS representative as to what information we wanted.

SIX

Admiral Baker explained that we would need help from the IRS in this next leg of the investigation and introduced us to Homer Johnson, the Assistant Director to the IRS. We relayed to him the daunting questions we had come up with. Johnson said he would instruct his agents that were going to work with us on this problem to make audits as we suggest. Baker asked to have a list of, or rather a copy of, each interview statement sent to each employee and each director, officer and any contract worker. Also, we needed to know if the income generated in each business increased after the new owners took over operation. Johnson said he would instruct his agents the audit was being done in conjunction with the Immigration Department to confirm that all employees are in the country legally and to confirm that all have reported wages properly.

We gave Johnson the information on the Henry cases five, six and eight. He said he would have IRS agents contact us within the next week. He would see to it that we each got the necessary ID as an IRS agent.

Thursday morning we had the three IRS agents come to our office. We had our usual coffee and donuts. We explained to them what we were trying to achieve. They agreed it sounded as if this would give us the information we wanted. The names of the three agents were John Clay, Barry Scott and Roland King. They gave us IRS I.D. badges and other necessary identification information.

Johnson wanted each of us D.I.A. agents to pair up with one IRS agent. I paired up with John Clay; Agent Jones would go with Barry Scott; Agent Small would go with Roland King; Agent Hope would stay in the office as a contact for each group.

As soon as he got back to Washington, Johnson sent a letter to each of the three cases notifying that an audit would be conducted in the next few weeks and all income statements and government reports should be available to the IRS agents when they reached their offices.

John Clay was the senior of these three agents so he elected to go on the first case which was Henry number five. I was to go with him on this audit. This was the barbeque restaurant owner. The main office for all of these was at the restaurant on Interstate 30 just before leaving Texas going east.

Clay and I arrived just after 9:00 a.m. on a Tuesday. Clay was well prepared to secure the information that we wanted; he had a calculator and an old copy machine. He said most of the time the people being audited were glad for us to use their copy machine, but sometimes they don't. His was for backup, and incredibly slow.

The office manager and accountant greeted us. They offered coffee and donuts and informed us we would have access to anything we needed to conduct the audit. After coffee and small talk, John asked to see copies of all of the W-2's for the past year.

"What do you need the W-2's for?" asked the accountant.

Clay looked him in the eye. "We need to check two things: first, to make sure the income was reported by each individual, and second, that each was in the country legally."

Both the office manager and the accountant seemed to get a little nervous.

"We are also going to need a list of all the stockholders and their dividends, as well as a list of the directors and their income. Are there any existing contracts with the employees or any consultants?" The red flag went up on this.

They said there were no contracts with employees. Nothing was said about contracts with consultants. We had to ask again and they said that there might be one.

Clay pinned him down for an answer.

"Okay, okay. We do have an agreement with one company to improve businesses." The office manager handed over a copy of the "agreement," as they called it, which was definitely a binding contract.

This contract was very unusual. First of all, the contract was with Golden Consultants with offices in Newark, New Jersey. The contract listed the average sale of products for three months prior to date of the contract. Golden Consultants would work three months for only one thousand dollars. If they increased business by 30% then they would extend the contract to be paid ten thousand dollars monthly as long as business was 30% over the stated figure that was average for the three months prior to signing. There was also to be paid to Golden Consultants 10% of the gross profits each year.

We kept a copy of the contract. Clay asked, "Did the profit increase?"

The manager said, "Greatly. The new owners improved business a lot on their own, and then ever since Golden Consultants was brought on the profits have really soared."

"Here are some papers we recently had notarized that shows the details of Golden Consultants being incorporated with our company." The manager handed over a stack of legal papers.

After looking it over, I noticed the name listed as the President of Golden Consultants was the same one that signed the original contract: Al Gotto. At the time, Clay and I did not recognize that name. Later on, we researched back ground history on him and found out that Al Gotto just so happened to be the big boss of the Mafia in New Jersey. It looks as if he may be expanding his operations.

The contracts and mailing address did not change. The change must have been because of the new law that exempted company dividends from income tax. It looked like the Mafia had found a way to launder drugs and other illegal money. It appeared there was so much money involved that in order to make income look legal they did not object paying a lot of income tax. Of course the new tax law on dividends will help them in getting a tax break on funds they take personally.

Clay said that a visit to the home office of Golden Consultants, Inc. was definitely going to be on our schedule. We first headed back to the office in Irving. We were eager to compare notes with the other agents on the other two Henry cases. This should be very interesting.

Agent Hope was busy with all the paperwork and needless government reports it takes to satisfy the political people in Washington. We had asked her to check with the FBI and get a list of all of the known associates of Al Gotto. She had contacted the FBI and they were reluctant to comply and make a list without proper authority. She also contacted Newark, New Jersey and the New York City police and asked for a list from them. New Jersey and New York agreed to comply.

Clay and I waited at the office working on the reports of our findings. We would soon be joined by Agents Jones, Scott, Small and King who were completing their audits.

Agent Jones and Scott were the first to join us around ten the next morning. Both were excited about what they had found and were anxious to relate this information to us.

They began their audit at the location that was shown to be their office and found this office was still in operation but the new location had been secured close to the county courthouse. The records for all operations were located at this new site.

Arriving at the new location Barry immediately asked to see W-2 forms for the past year and told the company manager they were checking on several things. Checks would be made to determine if all of the employees and stockholders were in this country legally and also to make certain each individual had reported all of their income. He also asked the manager to produce a list of all stockholders and officers of the company, their dividends, salary and bonus pay. He also wanted him to produce any contracts with the employees or with any consultants.

Agent Jones said at this point the auditor seemed to get a little nervous. He hesitated a few moments and said that they had a contract with a consultant and they had just received a certified notification informing them that the consulting company has changed to a corporation and the document listed the same individual that had been the consultant on the individual contract with the company. This document was signed by the president of the new company, Al Gotto, president of Golden Consultants. The auditor said they probably incorporated in order to take advantage of the new law that exempts dividends from being taxed. He said he had heard of a lot of small businesses, partnerships and individual business owners were doing the same thing in order to save tax dollars. Barry asked to see the contract with the consultant. Generally, it's pretty normal for the fee to the consultants to be based on the percentage of the increase in business. However, this one was a little unusual. They were signing a contract to work for three months. At the end of that time if they had increased business by 30% they would be paid one thousand dollars and the contract would be extended so they would be paid ten thousand dollars monthly as long as the business was 30% over the average that was stated for the three months prior to signing. The consultants were to be paid each year before taxes by the newly named company Golden Consultants. Golden Consultants were to take in 10% of the profit, before taxes, each year. The manager said this seemed to be a lot to pay for these services but that business had increased much more since getting this consultant.

Scott and Jones did not know what Clay and I had found on our audit. When we relayed our findings to them, they were surprised to learn the results from the two cases were almost identical. Neither of them had connected the president of the company, Al Gotto, to a tie in with the Mafia.

Agent Small and King came to the office just as Jones and Scott were completing the information about their Investigation into the Henry #8 case. Now to avoid repeating information, Small and King found the same findings from the Henry cases five and six that had surfaced on their audit of Henry #8.

We all agreed that the audit of Golden Consultants, Inc. was to be very interesting and would be next on the list. We thought it wise to contact Admiral Baker and let him know of the progress that we were making on this case. We told Baker about Agent Hope attempting to get a list from the FBI of the associates of Al Gotto. Baker has a lot of connections in Washington and suggested that he contact the FBI for a list of names of known associates of Al Gotto. He said he knew that the FBI had been trying for years to get information that would convict Al Gotto but that he was pretty sure he was smart enough in his dealings to avoid any of this. The FBI knew that he was the head man of the mob around New Jersey, but they did not know how extensive that really was. They knew Al Gotto was laundering money from illegal activities but could not prove anything. He always ran each bunch of cash through legal businesses even though it created a larger income tax burden. There was a lot of money coming into these businesses so they just paid the tax and were happy to stay out of trouble with the IRS and attempted to avoid anything that would wave a red flag for the FBI to get involved.

We thought if we had the names of Gotto's associates we could match these with payroll reports when we had completed the audit on Golden Consultants. We talked about who would do the audit in New Jersey. The chosen ones for the audit were Agents Hope, Clay and King. We knew from past experience that Admiral Baker would have the list of known associates of Al Gotto in a very short time.

Scott, Small, Jones and I would stay here in the office in Irving, Texas and run background checks and mini investigations of the names generated from the FBI's list. Mainly, we would check IRS reports and also check nationwide for any illegal violations. Also, we would check for trips in or out of the USA, especially to the Cayman Islands or Switzerland, known havens for hiding money acquired by illegal means. At each of the locations we would check for numbered bank accounts. It looked like things were beginning to develop. This was Thursday and it looked as if this would be a good time to make a weekend get-away.

Helen was off for three days. We got a sitter for the kids and went to visit our old college friends, Fred and Carolyn, who lived in Santa Monica, California at the time. We had met them for weekends in Las Vegas on several occasions in the past, and made arrangements to meet them yet again in Las Vegas. Fred was an investment banker and made a lot of money. We always talked about his work and some of the projects that he was working on at the time. He and Carolyn, both knew I worked for the D.I.A. but they know nothing more and thankfully they have never been too inquisitive.

When we were in Las Vegas the four of us had a great time. If was always good to be with long-time friends. We all did some gambling, mainly slot machines. When we played the slots, we always played machines that were close to and visible to the entrance to the casino. Sometimes we would win and sometimes we lost, never much in either case. It just seemed that the slots close to the entrance pay off at a better percentage than others in the casino. Gambling is fun, but the main reason we would go to Las Vegas was to see the shows. There were many good performances at all hours of the day or night.

We had a good time and returned home Sunday afternoon.

On Monday morning at the office we received the information we had asked for from the FBI. The list of the names of Al Gotto's associates was shorter than had been expected. Only seventeen names were on the list that the FBI thought were worth investigating. Before we started on these seventeen, we did our usual Monday morning ritual: office coffee and a discussion of the investigation.

First of all, it appeared as though the investors who loaned money to the victims and eventually become owners of the business after the death of the former owner had no association with each other. Our initial inclination was that there had to be a connection, but nothing we found had proved this.

Another item evident from the audit was the change in income. We were able to get income records before and after the victim's death, showing on average an increase of profit of 30-40% immediately after change in ownership in each of the cases audited. Seeing as there was not enough time for the income to increase 30-40% from mere change in ownership and business tactics, it would appear as though perhaps the former owners were not reporting a percentage of their profits received in cash. This would have decreased the amount they owed in taxes. The only logical explanation is that when the new owners took over, all forms of income were reported. Not only does this avoid the possibility of tax evasion and a mess with the IRS, it also reflects to the new owner how much profit the business was making. Three months after the change of ownership, Golden Consultants entered the picture and the income for each business increased 30-40% again.

We ended that discussion and had a necessary and required second and third cup of coffee in the office. Then we continued with our investigation into the lives of the seventeen known associates of Al Gotto provided by the FBI. We had determined earlier the new owners of the businesses we had checked did not have any connection with each other. However, after getting the list from the FBI of known associates of Al Gotto, all of these names showed on that list. We checked with the IRS and found a total of eight of the seventeen on the list had received income from Golden Consultants. This was on last year's report and before Golden consultants changed to a corporation.

The audit group from New Jersey came back in the office on Thursday morning and without delay shared their findings with us. It seemed the eight new owners that were listed on the FBI list had received large incomes from the company. It looked as if this was a legal company and had some good reasonable accounts. When Al Gotto took control of the various businesses through Golden Consultant, the rate of income produced was virtually unheard of. This was a successful business that had added a way to launder money. There were several employees taking a large share of income from the company; among these, Al Gotto, his wife and his children were listed on the payroll and receiving good salaries, director's fees, and very good dividend checks. They seemed to be taking full advantage of the new tax law to get some of this illegal money into their bank account without throwing up a red flag to the IRS.

There was one surprisingly unusual piece of information that showed up on the audit: Al Gotto and three other persons on the list did a lot of expensive travel. Mr. Gotto's trips were to Italy. One other made several trips to Italy. One showed several trips to Ecuador and one made several trips to New Caledonia in the South Pacific. After some discussion, we determined that we should monitor the activities of these three and also of Al Gotto. None of us believed in witchcraft or any weird cults, but it appeared as though the trips made out of the U.S. took place immediately prior to the deaths that we have investigated.

We released the IRS agents and thanked them for their help and all of us put forth our ideas on what to do next. Bottom line: surveillance of the four travelers was going to be necessary.

We called Admiral Baker and brought him up to date on our investigation. He said he would arrange a 24 hour observation on their activities. Based on the amount of salary they received from the company, it appeared as though Al Gotto and the other three men listed, Herman Chestnut, Boyce Kent and Justin Price, that traveled the most were the employees of highest status in the company. We were going to be on standby to follow up if they plan to leave the U.S.

We had made a lot of progress on these cases, but we still had not been able to determine the cause of death of the subjects in our Henry cases, or determine if the mafia was involved.

SEVEN

For many years most of the civilized nations in the world were members of the worldwide organization, the United Nations, they all worked together to capture criminals. Since the bombing of the World Trade Center in New York a new organization has been formed. This group was called World Net, the Nations friendly to the U.S. had become members and worked together to capture criminals and all suspected terrorists.

Italy and Ecuador were members of the World Net organization; we were going to have to utilize World Net in our pursuit of Al Gotto and his involvement in our cases.

New Caledonia is a small island in the Pacific Ocean, and was not associated with World Net. Admiral Baker said he would contact our state department and get the ball in motion to bring New Caledonia into the World Net for our purposes. Until then, we would have to focus our efforts on the activity in Italy and Ecuador.

We felt that the IDs we had established as insurance investigators for "Alton Insurance" would be acceptable in this new phase of our investigation.

We did not have any personal contact with any of these four that were now the main subject of our investigation. We felt one of these four would lead us to a clue into their involvement in the deaths of the subjects of the Henry cases.

Anytime we left the U.S. for cases abroad, it was protocol to have males and females pair up for the assignment together as to not draw attention. At the time, we had three male agents and one female, and thus needed two more female agents to join us. We requested the extra agents from Admiral Baker, and they were to report to us at the Irving office.

We had been doing routine work in the office for about a week when the new female agents reported to us. They immediately joined us in checking the background of Gotto, Chestnut, Price and Kent.

All of the four had numerous bank accounts, none of which showed anything illegal. All had valuable homes in New Jersey, New York (mainly in the Hamptons on Long Island) and in Palm Springs. Three of the four had additional valuable property in Florida.

Al Gotto also had property in Italy; however, we were unable to determine with our own resources the exact location in Italy. We contacted a World Net agent in Italy for his assistance in pinpointing the location of that additional property. We received reports daily from the agents who were monitoring the homes and calls of the four men.

No investigative trips out of the country were planned at this point in time. Until some suspicious activities came up as a result of the surveillance, we were to remain at the office in Irving.

EIGHT

Things were getting pretty dull in our office when we were called into the conference room for an emergency meeting with Admiral Baker.

"Thanks for gathering in here. I just received a call from the Immigration and Border Patrol post down in Laredo, Texas needing our help to catch drug smugglers from Mexico. I am sure that you are aware, Laredo is the main point of entry for drugs into the United States."

Agent Small asked, "How can we be of assistance to them?"

"The current method of checking each car as it reaches the border check point is effective, but time consuming. When a vehicle is detected to be transporting drugs, it backs up the entire line of traffic at the point of entry. They have requested our help in detecting smugglers, and also in helping to move the traffic along through the inspection station in a timely manner. I confirmed that we would send some agents to help, while informing them that we are in a stale point of our own investigation that could climax at any time. We will be able to leave Laredo at a moment's notice to pursue our assignment to apprehend the main suspects in the mafia ring. Now, we need to brainstorm on how this process can be effectively executed." Baker informed us.

We broke out into discussion of the best way to accomplish this new project and still be ready if something developed on our current project. We decided that Agent Hope and I would go to Laredo and be joined by the newly recruited agents that just joined us. These two, Theodore Norris and Helen Watson agreed with the plan. This would leave Agent Jones and Agent Small in the office in Irving, Texas and they could notify us if anything developed on the four people we were observing.

We contacted Immigration at Laredo and informed them that four of us would be coming down to assist them, and would arrive at 2:00 p.m. in one of the smaller government planes. They would have one of their agents meet us and escort us in an unmarked van to the main Immigration and Border Patrol office where we can determine what type of transportation we will need and then make arrangements for lodging.

This took the remainder of the day and we prepared to delve into the drug smuggling problem the next morning.

To make our jobs flexible we rented two cars from their motor pool. We booked four rooms at a local hotel so that we could easily get together after the workday to discuss the matter at hand.

When we arrived at the inspection station at the border crossing we were amazed by what we saw. There were eight lanes in each direction, and each lane was backed up as far as the eye could see, all day and night. The traffic jam that we witnessed would make those in New York City look like a minor event. What made it even worse was the fact that at least half of these vehicles that lined up for a long way were 18 Wheelers. Some people refer to them as "semis." Whatever you prefer to call them, it was a mess.

Before we could really get started, we could not forget the main case that we were working on. We placed a call to Irving to check with Agents Small and Jones to see if any new information had been received by them in the Irving office: nothing new so far.

We had been working with Immigration inspectors at the check point for a couple of days when Agent Watson made a suggestion for the problem they presented us with.

"What if we move the employee's parking lot just one lot further away from the check point? This would give us access to the employee lot so we could move suspicious vehicles to that location to complete the searches. That way, the backing up of traffic would be eliminated during inspection and would leave more accessibility for impounding a vehicle and arresting the occupants if need be."

The officer in charge, Tim Pinson, replied, "I had the same idea and actually submitted it to Washington two years ago. Washington stated that the employee lot could not be moved until the written procedure for handling drug searches gets amended."

We disagreed with the response, of course, and as any warm blooded government employee would do: informed security to switch the signs for the parking lots bump the employee lot one lot over, and park the closest lot to say "restricted parking" to show #2 parking for employees and #1 as restricted parking. I sent out a memo to the employees that the lots had been switched, and the change would take effect Monday. I also sent a memo to Washington showing the changes, and declared that we would assume all responsibility for the change. By the time Washington gets around to reading the memo, the change will already have been in practice for several days, and they would be able to see the benefits.

By noon on Monday, three separate vehicles had been effectively moved out of the line of traffic and onto the lot for further examination. It seemed that the access of the lot did help move traffic through the check point faster, but something else needed to be done. If only Mexican officials would check the vehicles before they reached the border crossing area.

After a couple of days of this new procedure Agent Norris voiced a new idea, "What if we used some sort of global tracking device (GTD) with a strong magnet to attach to suspected vehicles as they go through the inspection station? That way, local law enforcement officers in Texas can pick up the car and investigate it away from the border patrol station. That would eliminate any traffic blocks."

We discussed his plan and all agreed that it could work. From the point of entry of Laredo, most cars stay on Interstate 35 until they reach Oklahoma City, where they could then switch to Hwy 44 and then on to Hwy 55 and head on to Chicago. So, it appeared that the vehicle would get stopped on I-35 anywhere before reaching Oklahoma City. Norris contacted his friend, Ray O'Daniel, which worked in the FBI lab to see if they had a global tracking device that could be fitted with a magnet for our purposes. O'Daniel reported that they did have something that could work. They could just modify some existing GTDs to meet our needs.

We were in the middle of discussing where on I-35 would be a good location to intercept these vehicles when we were notified by FBI monitoring our four suspects in the main case that Chestnut had made reservations for a flight to Italy. We immediately notified World Net in Italy of the flight information and made arrangements for Norris and Watson to fly to Italy. Perhaps by the time they return to Laredo we will have an answer from O'Daniel. Agent Hope and I continued to work at the border crossing at Laredo.

Agents Norris and Watson had been gone for three days when we heard from them. Chestnut arrived in Italy and stayed in Rome for the duration of his stay. It appeared to be a normal social visit with family. He did meet with two businessmen on two different occasions, but the meetings were short and seemed innocent. The men did not appear to have any connections to one another other than through Chestnut. The World Net agents were to keep watch on him until he returned to the USA, and at the airport his luggage was to be checked thoroughly before boarding the plane. If Gotto's group was somehow causing the deaths of the subjects of the Henry cases, perhaps whatever they were using to cause such deaths was carried in their luggage. Norris and Watson made plans to return to Laredo on Thursday.

At the border crossing, we were finding suspicious vehicles at about the rate of one per hour. This continued on a 24 hour basis.

O'Daniel called and reported, "I have over 100 tracking devices left over from a previous job that would be easily modified to serve your needs. I'll be arriving with the devices on Monday, and will stay around to make sure everything works as planned."

Monday morning, the Laredo team convened around the meeting table in the conference room and indulged in coffee and the usual donuts.

Agent Watson relayed the details of the trip she and Norris just returned from. After a brief discussion, both Norris and Watson agreed that Chestnut could be eliminated from the list of prime suspects. We ended our discussion of the trip to Rome and got to work on the border crossing problem.

Traffic was moving better since we had moved some of the suspected vehicles to a parking lot to continue inspection and hold for legal action.

O'Daniel joined our meeting shortly after 9:00 a.m. He had been working with the FBI on special projects for several years. I was expecting O'Daniel to have many boxes with him, full of the tracking devices. However, that was not the case and I was surprised to see all he had with him was a briefcase and two medium sized cartons. He pulled one device out of his pocket that looked like three 25 cents quarters glued together. One of the discs, or quarters as we were calling them, was a strong magnet. The other was a global tracking device, and the third was a means of identifying the individual devise. He had one hundred discs in those small boxes. More than enough to get our tracking plan into action.

The other item he had was a receiver that would transmit the location and identification number of each device. He said that he would need to conduct a test run and find a location to set up a receiver. From our earlier discussion, we had decided that the cars would need to be intercepted along I-35. Agents Norris and Hope would leave with O'Daniel the following morning to travel up Interstate 35 to find locations for identifying receivers and for the best places for local law enforcement officers and state troopers to stop vehicles.

O'Daniel explained to us, "When you suspect a vehicle, you can attach a device to the radiator at the location where fluids leave to enter the motor. This could be done without attracting attention. You need to make sure to note the identification number of each device as well as the time of day it was placed on the car; the color, make, model and license plate of the vehicle it was placed on; and a description of the occupants and suspected location of illegal substance. The operator of the receiver would then notify a State Trooper of the vehicle's progress up I-35."

Watson and I stayed at the border crossing to continue working with the inspection team.

There was a State Trooper substation on the service road next to I-35 in Temple, which would serve as the first receiver location. O'Daniel, Norris and Hope stopped at the substation and explained the situation. The officer in charge was very helpful and agreed to help with problem. He further suggested three areas for state troopers to sit ready to grab the suspected vehicles for inspection: directly north and south of Waco, and also just south of Hillsboro.

The three agents returned to the border crossing at Laredo and gave the rest of us the "all clear" to begin the project.

All agreed that we would conduct a test run on one suspected vehicle to see how well this plan worked out before sticking the devices on multiple cars.

Early the next morning Norris found a good subject for our test run: an older couple, about fifty years old, driving a three year old tan Ford Explorer with indications of drugs behind the door panels. Agent O'Daniel secretly attached the global tracking device, GTD #37, to the lower part of the radiator next to the outlet that connects to the auto's motor. The Ford was released to enter the US. We immediately notified the control point in Temple of the identification number of the device and the necessary descriptions of the vehicle and its occupants.

The control operator informed us that GTD #37 was moving up on his indicator and that he would follow up and notify the trooper as it passed through Temple.

When we attached the GTD to the suspect's vehicle it was late in the afternoon. The operator positioned at Temple notified us that GTD #37 made a stop in San Antonio for food, and then continued on for about twenty minutes to stop at a hotel for the night. The suspects did not seem to be in any hurry to reach their destination. Of course, we did not know where they were planning to collect their payload.

The following day at approximately 2:00 p.m. the suspects passed through Temple. The State Trooper was notified and pulled over the car just north of Waco. Since we believed the couple to be transporting a large amount of illegal matter hidden in the door panels, we advised the trooper to request a backup. The trooper played it cool and looked around a bit before looking at the door panels. Sure enough, there were many bags of cocaine packed in the door panels.

The couple was placed in custody and the vehicle was towed to the nearest police garage in Waco. There, the drugs were removed under guard and placed in a secure compound.

After viewing this operation, we felt confident in trying this same procedure on average three times a week in order to relieve the load at the border.

O'Daniel said he would stay a few more days to make certain that everyone understood the operation. Norris, Hope, Watson and I left Laredo to go back to our office in Irving. We all felt that something new was about to develop.

When we got to the office in Irving we had a memo from Admiral Baker that stated he had been successful in getting New Caledonia to become a member of World Net and they were hiring and training people to work with them. This gave us contacts at all of the countries that we suspected Gotto, Kent and Price to be visiting. We suspected one of these three men must be obtaining some sort of unidentified poison or some other substance to cause death, from one of places they were visiting.

After two days of working on reports we were contacted by the FBI. They reported that Kent had made firm plans to go to Ecuador three days from now on the 17th of this month at 11:00am.

We sprang into action and contacted the World Net in Quito to brief them on our interest in Kent and his activities. A photo of him was forwarded to them, as well as any reports we had written involving him. Agents Small and Jones made arrangements to fly Quito before Kent would arrive. World Net said they would have agents meet Small and Jones at the airport on Thursday, the day before Kent was due to arrive. The agents would brief Small and Jones as to what the local police knew from past observations of the mafia affiliates. They would also set up agents to observe

Kent upon his arrival. Small and Jones boarded their flight, while Norris, Watson, Hope and I stayed behind in the Irving office.

It seemed the headquarters in Washington requested enough reports and paperwork to keep all of us busy any time we were at the office in Irving.

I contacted Admiral Baker and inquired if any more deaths that were labeled with the cause unknown had been reported to him.

Baker said, "Three new deaths had been reported in the last two months. I feel we were on the right track by following up on the information we had gathered."

I told him, "Agents Small and Jones were going to Ecuador to check on Boyce Kent who was due to arrive in Quito tomorrow."

"The border patrol at Laredo has been using the new system you had set up to help them move the traffic through the check point. They want you to come back if any new ideas were thought of," said Baker.

After I got off the wire with Baker, Agent Hope told me, "All the stops that the State Trooper made had determined that the big boys in the drug trade had hired drivers for just one trip. Also, more vehicles had been purchased recently using cash, and the titles of the vehicles were issued in the name of the drivers. The vehicles were all about four or five years old. They probably thought that newer ones would attract attention. Through interviews with the drivers while in custody, it was revealed that as part of the deal the drivers would keep the vehicles if the trip was a success".

While the method we were implementing was very successful, it was becoming a drag. I needed more entertainment and wondered if there was a way to continue being successful and have a little fun along the way as well. Hope was feeling the same way.

There was a separate group called "Special Forces" of the D.I.A. that was able to do just about anything. Agent Hope suggested that instead of having State Troopers stop the vehicles that had been tagged with the GTD devices we could have Special Forces follow and take several different actions. They could follow and when the suspect leaves the car unattended to eat or sleep for the night, Special Forces could steal their auto and deliver it to local police officers for inspection. Subjects would be confused and think that some stranger had stolen the car, but would be afraid to make a report because of what would turn up in the car once it was found. They would also be afraid to notify the boss who had hired them to deliver drugs. This would eliminate the suspects as a carrier of drugs. Also, we could ask Special Forces to have some type of vehicle that could cause an accident to the suspect's vehicle to make it impossible to drive. The wrecker would be called and the vehicle taken to the Patrol office to be inspected. Other variances could be carried out as well without letting the drug dealers know that it was a planned operation by the government. Norris suggested that we ask Special Forces to consider following the suspect to the point of delivery and see if they could catch some of the so called "Big Boys" (the major drug dealers). We agreed with the plan that Agent Hope had submitted and also the idea that Norris proposed.

I decided that it would be best if Norris and Hope went to Laredo to work with the Special Forces. Helen and I would stay at office in Irving and continue with reports and be available if anything new developed on the main investigation.

The FBI was still checking on the activity of Gotto and Price in the meantime. Something was bound to come up soon.

NINE

Agents Small and Jones were met in Quito by World Net agents. Boyce Kent was scheduled to arrive the next morning. The World Net agents had been very busy checking on Kent since we had contacted them.

It was discovered that Kent had a house in Quito, and his wife and three children lived there. His house was situated on seven or eight acres in a very good part of the city and looked much like something the movie stars living in the USA would have. The house had an eight foot tall masonry fence around the perimeter of the property. The fence had two separate metal gates with vertical bars about two inches apart: one for driving and one for walking through. These gates were for security measures and the bars were to keep animals out of the property. Many packs of wild dogs roamed the area. There were also security guards on the grounds at all times, and the family had several maids, cooks and gardeners.

The World Net agents said they had been checking on drug dealers and had determined that most of the drugs were being controlled by someone from within the USA. They had been working on determining who was controlling this operation and how they could eliminate him.

Agent Jones informed agent Small, "If Kent was in charge of the drugs operations he would be eliminated by the D.I.A." The agent seemed to think that Kent could very well be the head of the drugs group in Quito. They had done a lot of checking on him since they were notified that the D.I.A. was interested in him.

World Net had also been checking on the money flow into Kent's accounts. Several of the known dealers in the local drug trade had been making trips to the USA. The police in Quito did not have any way to check on their activity while the suspects were in the USA except through the World Net which allows for information to flow back and forth. They felt sure that there was a connection between the local drug dealers in Quito and Kent.

Agents Small and Jones worked with the local Quito agent who had been assigned to them from World Net. The World Net agents reported all the known drug dealers Kent was known to associate with, and described the typical meeting he would have with them at a desolate local restaurant. First, one car would drive up to the front of the restaurant and three or four members would get out and look around. Then, after fifteen minutes a driver would get in, move the car about twenty-five from the entrance. Shortly after that, another car would arrive and Boyce Kent and one other person would exit that car and enter the restaurant. This would be repeated with two more cars each having two passengers.

Agent Jones discussed this with the World Net agent to see if the time and location of the next meeting could be learned from World Net undercover agents. It was determined they would most likely meet up at the same restaurant. Efforts would be made to set up listening devices at this location. All agreed on this plan and World Net also said that it looked as if Kent was the kingpin of the drug trade and they would manage to get listening devices placed in his home.

Things were beginning to develop in Quito. Agent Small called the office in Irving and relayed the progress he and

Agent Jones were making with their observation of Kent. Watson talked with him and informed him that she and I were still working on the reports. Nothing had developed with Gotto or Price. Watson informed Small that Norris and Hope had gone back to Laredo to make more plans to help with the problems and that part of the entry into the USA. Plans that they had put into effect did nothing more than help to move traffic through that location. Something new had to be done to eliminate all of the drugs coming into the USA.

Special Forces liked the idea of following a vehicle that had been identified at the checkpoint. Marvin Loft was the agent in charge of the group from Special Forces who had arrived in Laredo to carry out this project. Loft said he would like to start by following a suspect to the end point where they would meet whoever it was to receive the drugs that were hidden in that car. He said he was almost certain the final destination of the vehicle from Mexico would be Chicago. The drugs would then probably be split up and sent to different directions. Loft said they had plenty of contacts with the local police who were also working on this drug problem. They had indications that drugs were being traded for firearms of all types and even some weapons that terrorists would like to be able to get their hands on.

It took a couple of days at the inspection site to locate a vehicle carrying drugs and Loft thought it would make the trip all the way to the exchange point in Chicago. The vehicle was a five year old Ford four door sedan. Other than the slightly faded paint, it appeared to be in good condition. It was driven by a couple probably in their early fifties.

It appeared they had hidden drugs behind every door panel. The GTD was attached to the exit contact of the radiator. The vehicle was given a clear pass, and nothing was done to make the driver think that we suspected anything. The description of the vehicle, Mexican plate number, and brief description of the two people who would be in the car were charted and the information fed into the computer. Loft had two of his agents ready to follow.

It wasn't necessary to follow close behind the suspect's car because of the GTD device. However, they did need to be within five or ten miles of the suspects so agents could observe when they made a stop. These two agents were both Polish and had last names that were really hard to pronounce, so, we always called them by their first names, Pete and Oscar. Of the two, Oscar seemed to be the one to naturally take charge.

Back in Quito, Small and Jones were beginning to get results from the listening devices they had installed to observe Kent. It seemed Kent had been talking with contacts in Guayaquil (pronounced *Gwyah-keel*), Ecuador's principal seaport. Not only was Kent living the life of luxury when he was in Quito but he also owned a very expensive helicopter that was going to be used for his visit to Guayaquil. It turned out that after investigation by World Net the helicopter was leased to him each time he was in Quito. It would appear he would probably be making visits to other cities during his time in Ecuador.

The World Net agent in Quito made contact with agents in Guayaquil and told them that he and two D.I.A. agents from USA were on the way to the city. He informed them as to what they were looking for: mainly, to find out to what degree, Boyce Kent was involved in the drug trade.

Of course, Small and Jones were checking to see if he in any way was obtaining anything that could kill a person without leaving a clue as to what caused the death. It already seemed very evident to Jones that Kent was very much involved in the drug trade, but was he also the one smuggling the poison to the US? So far, there have been no clues as to where the poison was coming from. They did not think Kent to be the carrier. It appeared he was mainly interested in the drug trade.

We made the trip to Guayaquil and were met by their World Net agents. Kent had a meeting planned at a local restaurant. World Net had agents install the listening devices in place. They were very efficient. The meeting Kent conducted confirmed that he was the number one man in the drug trade. Agents Small and Jones assured the World Net agent that the D.I.A. and U.S.A. would be certain justice would be done in the case of Kent. Kent was leaving Ecuador on Thursday. Agent Small notified the immigration officials in New York airport to make a close inspection of Kent's luggage. They would notify us if anything unusual develops. They had previously been informed as to items we were trying to locate. Mainly we were looking for anything in medicine bottles or tablets that did not appear to agree with the label that identified the medicine.

Agents Small and Jones were on the same plane with Kent on the trip back to the U.S.A. Nothing developed at the airport inspection. The two agents felt discouraged because they were not able to link Kent with the crimes. Small and Jones made connections with a flight back to the DFW airport in Texas, so they could return to the office in Irving and report on all that had transpired.

TEN

Monday morning found Small and Jones in the office when Helen and I arrived. We had the usual government coffee and briefed each other on activities we had been involved in the past two weeks.

Pete and Oscar were following a vehicle that had been identified as having a substantial amount of drugs hidden in the door panels. A GTD had been attached and the two occupants did not know they were suspected of doing anything illegal.

The first stop was just south of San Antonio at a fast food restaurant. They stayed there just long enough for a restroom break and a burger and drink. Their next stop was another fast food restaurant at Salado. It appeared that these stops were pre-determined. Both of these were close to the exit from the interstate. Also at Salado, they checked in at a nearby motel. Pete and Oscar also checked in at the same motel. Oscar said normally they would select a different motel, but this was the only one in this area that had a vacancy. After the agents checked in at the motel, they called a control number in Temple and asked to be notified if the suspects changed locations.

The next morning the suspects had breakfast at the same fast food restaurant across the interstate from the motel then headed north again. The agents followed and all the stops were real close to freeway exits. This pattern continued all the way to Chicago. The locations of their stops were definitely predetermined. Chicago agents had been notified when the suspects were within one hundred miles of their city so they had plenty of agents on alert by the time the suspects reached the city. The agents in charge of the locator device tracked the vehicle and kept their agents informed. The agents followed and watched the suspects in case they entered a garage.

After they followed the suspects for a short time, the suspects exited the freeway and went about six blocks to a supermarket parking lot. They stopped and parked as soon as they could after entering the parking area. This gave the agents a good opportunity to locate where they could observe and be ready to move in if the subjects made contact with a local group. This situation remained the same for about two hours.

Finally a black car with darkened windows drove by the suspects' car, then around the parking lot area, then back by the suspects where it parked five parking spaces down from the suspects' car.

The agents kept a keen eye on this new player, and after about thirty minutes another black car with dark windows came on the parking lot and drove up next to the car of the suspects from Mexico.

When all of the precautions were taken by the occupants of the two black cars, our agents felt that a transfer was about to take place.

One person got out of the black car closest to the suspects' car and motioned to the other black car to approach. As they came near the GTD car, the suspect got out and was about to enter the black car when our agents decided to act. All of the vehicles were surrounded and the occupants captured.

It turned out the suspects were just local thugs that worked for the big boys who controlled the drug trade. After taking all of the players to the local police substation, it didn't take long to get information about who the big boys were, and how we could locate them.

The plan was to have one person from their gang take the suspects' vehicle to the shop to remove the drugs from the door panels and then return the car to the suspects who would be waiting in a motel for the return of the car. Information supplied by the local thugs was enough to give the District Attorney cause to issue a warrant.

Pete and Oscar felt that this would help to slow down the movement of illegal drugs into the area.

Back at the Irving office, things were pretty well routine. Watson and I were now joined by Small and Jones back from their trip to Quito. The agents were working on the necessary paperwork when Norris and Hope walked in from their project in Laredo. Hope said they had marked another suspect car in the border crossing. They planned to observe and see if it made the same stops along the way as the one that they followed all the way to Chicago. It was determined it would be intercepted about one hundred miles before reaching Chicago.

After a few days we received word that Gotto had made reservations to go to Italy. This was good news because we were at a standstill in the case until we got some movement from Gotto or Price. After some discussion, it was decided that Small and Hope would make the trip to Italy to observe Gotto. This would leave Jones, Norris, Watson, and I at the office in Irving. We were still keeping an eye on the action at the border crossing at Laredo.

We had just heard from Admiral Baker that there was some underhanded operation going on in connection with the building of a submarine for the U.S involving money, material, and construction plans. Nothing was firm on this yet. Baker just wanted to alert us as to what was coming next. We briefed Baker on our slow progress on the case we were working on with the insurance policies. Admiral Baker fully understood that the investigation takes time, and he said that it looked as if this one would be completed soon after we completed our observations of the two remaining suspects.

Agents Small and Hope made preparations to leave for Rome, Italy. Small contacted the World Net agents in Rome and alerted them to prepare to assist us in observing the actions of Gotto while in Rome.

Listening to the conversations from the phone tap on Gotto's phone, it did not appear that he would be going anywhere in Italy except for the city of Rome.

Small and Hope arrived in Rome well ahead of Gotto. The World Net agents were well aware of Gotto. They knew what room he preferred in his favorite hotel and several other locations that were usually visited by him when in Rome. The agent had placed listening devices in a number of these locations so we'd get a pretty good idea of what was taking place and if anything unusual was happening

Shortly after Gotto arrived and settled into his rooms at the hotel, several different people began to come to his room for meetings. All of these visitors were well known to the World Net agents.

Late in the day the meetings stopped. No more activity until after nine p.m. when Gotto left and went to his favorite Roman restaurant. He had a private dining room and the other known affiliates jointed him there. This was one of the known places that he visited, so we already had listening devices in place. All of the conversation confirmed what was already known: Gotto was the top dog in the drug industry. Not only drugs, but he was involved in a lot of other illegal activity as well.

This routine continued for four days; meetings in the hotel with several people, then with a different group each evening. He seemed to have a large group of people tied in with his activities.

He prepared to leave on the fourth day. We notified Immigration to make a thorough search of his baggage when he arrived in the U.S. We told them to look for anything that looked as if it could be any type of poison, but not to let Gotto know that the search was anything out of the ordinary.

Small and Hope headed back to the U.S. and immediately checked with customs to see if anything was located during their inspection of Gotto. It turned out as we had suspected: nothing unusual. It seemed that all we had done so far was eliminate suspects, which left just one to be investigated: Justin Price. If observing him did not come up with a solution, then we were back to square one.

Small and Hope made it back to the office and were relating information from the trip to Italy with Jones, Norris, Watson, and me. After the meeting was over we all agreed that Gotto was not the one that had been smuggling in the poison that had killed the insurance victims. We also thought we should start an investigation about the submarine construction scam that Admiral Baker had briefed us about.

A call came in from Baker requesting that some of us go back to the Mexican border to attempt to transport illegal people through a point of entry. A large number of illegal immigrants had been brought in the states hidden in freight trailers. Of course, thoroughly checking all freight trucks is near impossible because it is so time consuming. As a result, some do get past customs undetected with illegal immigrants hidden within. Sadly, those hidden are often dead on passage from the lack of food, water, oxygen and heat.

I was selected to go to Laredo and Agent Hope accompanied me. As we were completing this discussion a call came in from the agent checking the activities of Justin

Price who had made plans to go to Noumea, New Caledonia, on Tuesday the 14th. The agent reported that Price had scheduled a meeting first thing Wednesday morning and mentioned something about going to Banika Island.

ELEVEN

Since there were only a few days before Price was expected to be in Noumea on the 14th, we decided that Agents Jones and Norris would take this assignment and leave as soon as possible and have time to notify and visit with New World agents in Noumea. It was good that Admiral Baker had made contact with the authorities in New Caledonia when he did a few weeks ago. Because of this, we had contacts established there.

Norris and Jones found out right away that there was only one flight weekly to that area of the South Pacific. That one flight left from LAX and landed in Guadalcanal, then made a shuttle flight to Noumea. This would terminate on the 13th. If they had chosen that route, they would be on the same plane with Price. Other plans were made to get Agent Jones and Theodore there before Price arrived. This way, they could talk with World Net agents and perhaps find out why Price was going to Banika Island.

Norris and Jones left DFW fairly close to the scheduled departure time. They made connections at LAX for a flight to Hawaii. After being airborne for about thirty minutes the captain came on the speaker and announced that, although departure was a little late, they would be arriving at LAX on time. He said the weather at Los Angeles was great, and that most of the flights were on schedule. The flight to LAX was uneventful and was on time, as the captain had stated that it would be. Rather than just sit and wait to board the flight to Hawaii, Norris took a walk up and down the long walkway between terminals. Jones found a paperback novel she had been wanting. They boarded the plane for Hawaii. It appeared that most of the passengers were headed for a holiday. It seemed that maybe half already were wearing Hawaiian shirts.

The passengers were loud and excited. The entire trip from LAX to Hawaii was very noisy. Norris and Jones were glad when they landed in Hawaii and departed to make connections for the flight to American Samoa. Everything was on schedule, which was very unusual. Both Norris and Jones had a nap because these passengers were very quiet. Guess they got rid of most of the party group while in Hawaii, about three-fourths of the way to Samoa.

The flight attendant announced that they were passing the equator. This brought back memories to Norris. His father was an American, and worked for the American embassy in Australia. His level of job allowed for his family to live there also. The family was provided transportation back to the U.S.A. once every two years. Norris remembered when they crossed the equator in those days the looked as though flight attendant always made a little speech. She said that before crossing the equator you were a "polliwog." She went on to describe the ceremony that took place aboard ship when they crossed the equator. He couldn't remember all of it, but he did remember something about they mentioned Davy Jones' Locker. Anyway, after crossing the equator you became a "shell back."

The rest of the flight to Samoa was uneventful: had a smooth landing and the layover to Noumea was three hours. Norris took a short walk away from the airport and encountered native Samoans who offered to climb coconut trees and break open coconuts for juice. Or milk, as they called it. He declined because he remembered some of the stories that were told by sailors from World War II: coconut milk was a cure for constipation. In fact, if you were normal, this would give you diarrhea. Several of the male passengers waiting for the flight to New Caledonia were observing the natives climbing the tree. Norris related to them the story he had heard from a veteran friend who was on a troop ship in World War II. To make this simple, Norris's friend will be "A" and the other veteran, "B." Both of these were on a troop ship that stopped at Pago Pago, Samoa. Some of the troops were allowed to go ashore. A and B were among that group. B did partake of some of the coconut milk. B also got seasick anytime the sea got real calm and glassy-looking. The morning of the second day after leaving Pago Pago, B got real sick and also had a bad case of diarrhea. The bathroom—or "the head," as the Navy called it—had commodes lined up in a row with no dividers in between. A knew that B was sick and in the bathroom, so when General Quarters was sounded, which meant that everyone should go up on deck, because of possibility of attack by submarine, seasickness is just as sick as you can get and not die. After the alarm sounded, A found his buddy B in the bathroom. He was sitting on one commode and throwing up into the other one. A hollered to him and said that General Quarters had been sounded. No answer. A hollered at him again and told him that he needed to go up on deck, that the ship might get torpedoed. B's reply was, "I sure hope so."

The trip from Samoa to Noumea, New Caledonia, was uneventful. Upon landing, they were met by a member of World Net named Edward Hoffmann. He had been briefed as to the subject of our investigation, Justin Price. Hoffmann briefly disclosed their investigation since receiving notice that World Net agents in the U.S. were interested in Price's activities in New Caledonia. He said that Price had visited their country about every six months for the past four years. It looked as though there was something happening during these visits that could help in solving these cases, where death was caused, and the cause was unknown. Agent Jones told Hoffmann that she was really tired from the trip, and the time change from the Irving area didn't help either. She was ready for some rest, and asked if she and Norris could meet with him at ten a.m. the next day. Hoffmann agreed, saying he had made the same trip as they had, on two different occasions and fully understood how tired they were. Hoffmann said he would meet them the coffee shop near their hotel.

The next morning, Hoffmann was already in the coffee shop, and had just started on his second cup of coffee when Norris and Jones came in. Hoffmann thought they looked ten years younger than they did the night before. It was really a hard trip they had completed. They had crossed three time zones—you could say almost four, since one time zone cuts across the northern part of New Caledonia.

Norris told Hoffmann that Price was involved in mafia activity in the U.S.A. Price was one of the leaders that controlled a lot of the drugs distribution. The group was also involved in many other illegal activities, some of which included murder. The World Net in the U.S. wanted to know exactly what Price was doing while outside the U.S. Agent Jones told Hoffmann that World Net agents had been observing Price's activity, and also listening in on telephone conversations, both at his home and his office.

When they heard that he was going to make a trip to New Caledonia, he also mentioned something about a week's stay on the island of Banika. It wasn't clear to those listening to his conversation, but as best as they could determine, he had said "Banika." Norris said they had checked and Banika was an island in the Russell group of the Solomon Islands. This island had not been developed for tourists. As best as could be determined, Banika was occupied by Japan in World War II. The Japanese left as the U.S. forces came ashore in 1943. However, the Japanese continued to bomb Banika as U.S. forces built airports, roads, and docks. Unlike many of the Islands, deep water was close to shore, so after they built docks, large freight ships could unload there. These large freighters would unload materials to store in warehouses that the Army and Navy had built. Then smaller ships could be loaded to take cargo on north where it was needed. The cargo transferred there consisted mostly of ammunition and gasoline drums. The Navy Seabees had crews that worked around the clock to make sure everything ran smoothly.

Banika was a coconut plantation owned by the Russell Islands Plantations Estates, Limited, that had not yet been developed to encourage tourism. Hoffmann said that it was highly unlikely that Banika was the location that Price was going to and that it must have been misunderstood. There's an island about thirty-five miles southwest of New Caledonia that had a similar name as Banika called "Bonita," and they would take tourists for one week at a time. They only accepted ten people per week and it was extremely expensive. Hoffmann said it would be difficult to determine if Price had actually been to Bonita Island. Chester Upchurch owns this island and the boats and the freight barges that travel from Noumea to Bonita Island. No other vessels were permitted to enter their harbor. Also, at their office in Noumea, after a group left Noumea for a week's stay at the island, there was not a record that showed the names of those that went on the tour. Agent Jones asked how it was possible for Upchurch to run his business without having to keep records of his visitors and Hoffman told him that Upchurch could do just about anything that he wanted because he owned the Island, and it was no longer claimed by any country. People who have made this week-long trip say that Upchurch explains how he happened to own this island. This explanation was delivered when they would first arrive at the island.

Norris and Jones had arrived in Noumea far enough in advance of the arrival of Justin Price so they could go to the airport with Hoffmann and observe Price's arrival. Hoffmann wanted to see if any of the local known criminals met him.

His arrival was uneventful. He was met by two men who accompanied him directly to the hotel. Neither of the two men was known to Hoffmann.

World Net had determined that Upchurch made two speeches to the group that was making a week-long trip. The first took place at their office in Noumea, and the second upon their arrival at Bonita Island. Hoffmann said that it would be very difficult to observe the meeting on the island, but after our talk last night they had been able to get a listening device placed in the office where the Wednesday meeting would take place.

Hoffmann left Norris and Jones to tour the town as they wished, and planned to meet at the World Net offices Wednesday in time to observe what was said at the meeting that Upchurch was to have with the group that were going to his island next Monday.

Norris and Jones took advantage to see some of the sights in Noumea, and had a late evening meal at a café overlooking the harbor.

Wednesday morning they met Hoffmann at the World Net Office. The group that was going to Bonita Island on Monday had assembled for the greeting speech from Upchurch.

The monitored conversation consisted mainly of small talk. A request for silence was made, and a young lady introduced Upchurch.

Upchurch made a few unimportant comments and then started a long speech, "Greetings to all of you who have reservations for next Monday to visit the island of Bonita. I ask that you remember to arrive on time when we have our second meeting this upcoming Wednesday. In the past, our visitors had a hard time overcoming jet lag and were furthermore distracted by the beautiful weather and skipped out or arrived late for the meeting.

"The scheduled departure time is 10:00 a.m. Monday. You will all return here 5:00 p.m. Saturday. Now, when you originally made reservations with us, you were requested to wire money to our bank here in Noumea a deposit for the sum of one thousand dollars. I would like to thank each one of you for complying with that, and would also like to remind you that the deposit is non-refundable.

"Now, let me relay to you some of the rules that apply to everyone visiting our island." Upchurch signaled to the lady that introduced him to pass out papers listing the rules for everyone to follow along. "Hopefully, you will recognize these rules, as they are the same ones sent to you when you booked your reservation.

"While on the island, you will not have in your possession any of the following: cell phones, lap tops, iPads, cameras, or anything else electronic. You may not have on your person, at any time, tobacco, alcohol, or any street drugs. You may take with you prescription medicine. However, the prescription must be in a labeled container that describes the medicine. For example, if your prescription is for Aricept, 5 milligrams, the round white tablet, side one should read: Aricept, side two give the dosage amount: 5mg. If your medicine is not clearly labeled, it will not be permitted on the island. All of you were notified of this prior to making reservations.

"Before you leave here on Monday, you will be asked to sign an agreement to these things. We will then make a thorough inspection of all your bags. Also, you are not permitted to bring any food or food supplements with you. Neither can you depart from our island with any food or drink. I want to make one thing very clear: the island is not a possession of any country; therefore my employees and I are the government there. This will be explained to you in the first meeting on Monday on Bonita Island. If you agree with these things that I have related to you and wish to proceed, kindly notify your bank to wire ten thousand dollars in the same manner that you sent the deposit. This should be done by closing time here in Noumea on Friday.

"Remember, we make no exceptions to any of our rules. We're glad you're here and hope that you will have a very satisfying experience. Just remember that our rules are reasonable and they will be observed." This concluded the speech by Chester Upchurch. The group of ten dispersed. There were a few comments about alcohol not being allowed on the island, and a group decided to hit the bar now to get it out of their systems now.

Jones suggested that Norris see about making reservations to go to the island for a week.

Hoffmann was not known by the public as an agent of World Net. All of his friends knew that he worked for the government, but they thought he checked for fraud in government agencies. Because of that, if was safe for Hoffmann, Norris, and Hope to be seen together. It would appear to anyone that Hoffmann was visiting with two tourists from the U.S.A. Since there was no problem being together in public, they decided to have lunch together and discuss what they had heard this morning. It appeared that Upchurch had some rules that had to be observed. He was firm about obeying the rules, but nothing was said as to what would happen if they weren't observed. Hoffmann said that one time he heard a guest was returned to Noumea in the middle of the night and sent on a plane leaving back to his home in New Zealand. Upon investigating the whereabouts of that guest, no record or information could be found as to what happened to the guest went after arriving in New Zealand.

After a discussion as to what had been learned from listening to the speech it was decided a trip to the island was absolutely necessary. Hoffmann had many other projects going on at the time and was eliminated as far as being the one to go to the island of Bonita to see if the source of poison could be determined.

Norris suggested that Jones would be the one to make the weeklong trip to the island that way he could stay in Noumea and work with Hoffmann to see if the United States had any information on some of the bad characters in the Noumea area. The I.D. that Norris and Jones carried showed that they were insurance investigators, and it appeared that they were here in Noumea on a vacation.

Agent Jones made the necessary application and was immediately accepted for the tour leaving that Monday. She was the last one to get a space for that week. She was told to be at their office Wednesday for the next meeting, and was given the list of island rules. They requested that her bank wire a deposit of one thousand dollars to their bank in Noumea before Wednesday morning. Agent Jones said that she could give them a check for the thousand dollars now. They said they did not accept any checks; the money must be wired. After that deposit is received, the sum of ten thousand dollars must be transferred by the same method by the close of business on Friday.

She was also given a list of clothing that would be needed. About the only things on the list that she didn't have were blue jeans, hiking and western boots. The lady at the office told Agent Jones where these items could be purchased. She also stated that it would be a good idea to wear each pair of the boots and try to get them what she called "broken in."

All that had to be done now was to get an approval from Admiral Baker for the cost of the trip to Bonita and subsequently to have the bank wire the money transfers. After relaying what they knew about Price, Admiral Baker said it looked as if the source of the poison used to kill the insurance policy holders without any known cause would soon be discovered. He agreed that Agent Jones was the logical one to go to Bonita and requested an update after she returned from the weeklong stay.

Hoffmann, Norris, and Jones thought it would be ideal if another trip could be planned so they could monitor the speech Upchurch would give to the ten new visitors, but it was not possible. Jones remembered that Norris's friend, O'Daniel had talked about a new surveillance device they were trying to develop that would be able to monitor a conversation by using a space satellite, similar to the way cell phones are used. Even if they already had developed this method, it could not be used here. It required that a definite global position be established. If that device was developed, and we had a global position, then conversation could be picked up and it would be as clear as listening on a cell phone. That plan was out for the time being, but all three enjoyed talking about that product being developed.

Agent Jones left the men to do her shopping for the visit to Bonita Island on Monday. She would still have to make the meeting on Wednesday. Hoffmann and Norris went back to the World Net office to see if any other information had been received from contacts in the United States. Nothing new had developed.

Norris told Hoffmann there were some locations he would like to visit while Jones was on the island for a week: Guadalcanal, Tugaghi, Iron Bottom Bay, and maybe, if time permitted, as far north as Bonika Island. He said that he also would like to visit Bougainville, but felt sure he would not have time to go that far. Hoffmann said he had a friend, John Fuller, who owned a plane that delivered fresh produce to some of the islands in that area. He made deliveries on Mondays, Wednesdays, and Fridays. Fuller sometimes took guests along on the deliveries because he enjoyed having someone go along with him on the ride. Hoffmann made an arrangement for Norris to go with Watson on the Friday route.

The two of them—Norris and Hoffmann—met up with Jones later in the day. Jones had found everything that she needed: western boots, hiking boots, blue jeans, and a jacket. She even had time to go to the Laundromat to wash and dry her pants and jacket to take the stiffness out of them. She seemed to think she had everything she needed for the weeks stay at Bonita Island. She said she was going to alternate wearing the pairs of boots each day until Monday to break them in.

Nothing of any importance happened until Friday morning, when Norris met Fuller at his private landing strip. They left Noumea at five a.m., with the first stop being Henderson Airport, on the north side of Guadalcanal. This was a short stop, picking up some tractor parts that were going to Pavuvu Island. The next stop after leaving Henderson Field was Tulaghi. This flight path was over Iron Bottom Sound. The outlines of several sunken ships could be seen from the air. There was a lot of activity at Guadalcanal, Tulaghi, and Iron Bottom Sound during World War II.

They stayed a short while at Tulaghi, and then flew to Bueno Vista Island to drop off some medical supplies. The next stop was Pavuvu Island and along the way they passed right over Banika Island. Both of these were among the Russell Islands. Norris wished they could have landed and spent some time at Banika. Among other things, John F. Kennedy was based in that area in World War II. Maybe this visit could be on another trip. Anyway, this was a good experience for Norris.

They got back to Noumea about one hour before dark. Agent Jones had been busy seeing the sights and breaking in the hiking boots. There was nothing much to report for Saturday and Sunday.

Monday morning was an exciting time for Agent Jones. She joined the group of nine people that were assembled and ready to board the Bonita Island transport ship for the thirty-five mile trip to the island. All of the people were early and eager to get started at the scheduled departure time of ten a.m. Agent Jones said that she would really like to make a tape recording of everything that was going to take place during this week-long stay at Bonita Island. The idea was quickly struck down because of the restrictions placed on the visitors due to the prohibition of any electronic devices. Jones promised to relate everything that happened during the week as soon as she got back.

The ten visitors and crew boarded and left for the island shortly after 10 a.m. Later, as Jones recalled the events, the thirty-five mile trip was uneventful. The weather was beautiful and the sea was smooth. They announced over the speaker that this was normal during the dry season. They even added a little humor by saying that during the dry season it rained every day, and during the wet season it rained all day every day.

They docked in a cove that had cliffs on either side that appeared to be at least a hundred feet tall. The dock area extended approximately one thousand feet, which was most of the area that made a long slope down to the water's edge. The construction of the dock and the building in that area was suburb. It looked like something you would see in a movie set or a dock area for the super-rich.

On landing, all were taken to a building that had several rooms, and one large room that looked more like the lobby of a very expensive hotel. There they were told it was time to inspect luggage and personal items to be certain no restricted items had been brought to their island. This went very smoothly except for one lady that brought two cartons of cigarettes, a camera, and a cell phone. The lady offered the inspector several hundred dollar bills to forget what they had found. He ignored her offer and calmly made a call to Upchurch. He then requested the lady wait in another room until Mr. Upchurch could arrive. Agent Jones and the other eight never saw the woman again. Later, they found out that she had been escorted off the island and all of her luggage was sent back to Noumea.

Agent Jones and the others were enjoying coffee and talking about how Upchurch had developed such a beautiful place. So far they had only seen the dock area and the adjacent buildings.

Soon Upchurch joined them and said the following, "When we talked with all of you on Wednesday, you were told that we would explain some things to you on Monday. First of all, some of you have stated that a total outlay of eleven thousand dollars for a six-day, five-night visit to our island seems a bit steep. You should know that you will experience something money cannot buy anywhere else.

"As I am sure you have already figured out, it is not possible for you to be contacted by anyone who is not on our island. Neither will you be able to communicate with them. We are completely isolated from the outside world.

"I will now explain, since some of you have asked, how I came to own and develop this island. My great, great grandfather was a cattle rancher and had two very large ranches. One was in the Midland, Texas, area and the other was in northwest Texas, close to a little community called Whiteface. He died suddenly and his only child, a son, had to take over the operation of these ranches at the age of seventeen. He had two very, very good years in 1890, so he bought stock in oil, railroads, and steel. All of his offspring were males, and each one was an only child. I was the last in line. My father died while in the Navy, when I was 22. So everything came to me.

"Now the old homestead was still standing and had been occupied by my foreman. I had received a very good offer to purchase some land that included the old homestead. The offer was accepted and I went to the house to see if anything needed to be salvaged. There was an old safe that everyone had forgotten about. I had to get a specialist to open the safe. There were a great many interesting things that were found while we were inventorying the contents of the safe. We found stock certificates to a gold mine. I really thought we had hit it big. Then I found out the gold mine had gone broke. The most amazing items that surfaced were stock certificates dated 1890. This was two years after my grandfather had assumed responsibility for running both of the ranches. And these stock certificates included oil, railroad, and steel. While checking on the stock certificates, we found that some had merged with others, some had bought other companies, and some had just gotten to be huge companies. And there were also some that had gone broke. The corporate offices of some of these companies were shocked. They were shocked to know that shares of stock had finally surfaced. They thought they had been lost forever.

"What was amazing was the total value of the stock. I am not going to reveal the total amount, but I will say that if all of Texas and Oklahoma were for sale, I could probably buy it. The funds were placed in trust by me, and for me. Some was to go for medical research, to colleges and to charities. This is when I came to the Pacific Ocean and found the island. It just so happens that at that time some of the countries in Europe were divesting themselves of small possessions in the Pacific. I bought this island and brought in engineers, land planners, and construction specialists. Most of the island is two hundred feet above sea level, with rugged cliffs right down to the water except for one cove or bay area, which is where we located the dock and operations center. Soon after we started having tourists stay.

"Everything that you should need while on the island has been provided for you. Since this island was purchased individually, we are not responsible to any nation. We have one law: ours. You have already been told that there will be no tobacco, alcohol, drugs, cell phones, nothing electronic, no beepers, cameras, and so forth. You will have no contact with the outside world until you return to Noumea on Saturday. If you violate any of our laws you will be dealt with at that time. I assume that each of you have observed that of the ten who arrived here this morning, there is now a total of nine in the group. Some people have a difficult time understanding the rules that we operate by here on the island be the total number in your group for the week. If, at this time, you do not agree with the rules that have been stated to you, please indicate now and you will be immediately returned to Noumea.

"Should you have any questions, Mr. Albert James, the agent in charge of your stay here, will be happy to discuss them with you. He will assign your cottage and someone will escort you there.

"Now, before you depart from this first meeting, I want to be sure that I have your undivided attention. I've told you of several of our rules. One of these pertains to food. None is to be brought onto this island by you, and none shall accompany you when you leave here. All of our food originates here, except for some staple items, seafood, and a few items that we cannot produce here. You're free to eat any fruit on this island, except one at certain times. Due to our climate you will find on most of the fruit trees new growth and also ripe fruit at the same time. Now I want each and every one of you to be sure that you listen to this: There is one fruit, which we call 'Rainbow Ball'—when this fruit develops it is green, about the color of a lime, and as it ripens, it changes to white. The pulp juice is also white at that time. Now when ripe and edible, it turns to orange. This ripe Rainbow Ball is better than any orange you have ever tasted. Perhaps you're thinking, 'Why is he talking so much about one type of fruit?' There is a very good reason. As I stated earlier, you are free to eat any fruit except the Rainbow Ball. This can only be eaten when the color is orange. Do not even think about tasting while in the white stage of ripening. One bite of white fruit or just two drops of juice will kill you in twenty-four hours. Before it is ripe, the pulp and the juice have no taste. The juice is clear as water. You will not get sick or feel any effects if you wish to test the truth of my statement. You will just die. If this happens, your body will be disposed of here, and there will not be any record of you having been here.

"If you have any questions, now is a good time to get the answers. Otherwise, Mr. James will see that you get to your cottage and get settled."

Before leaving for their cottages, Albert James told the group a little about the people that lived on the island. "By now, I believe you all have seen four or five island natives. You have also seen the staff, including myself and Upchurch. You might have noticed that there are not many differing body types out here. We are all extremely healthy. Our blood pressure, cholesterol, and blood sugar levels are well within the limits set by health guidelines. We are all within our 'ideal' weights; diabetes is unheard of here. In fact, a couple of medical universities and a research laboratory have conducted tests here to find out why we are so healthy. There will be more on that later."

He continued, "Let me get each of you to your cottage and then we will assemble for lunch and tell you about the afternoon plans." Everyone then boarded a small bus.

They had driven about two miles when they saw a building that was described as a recreational building which also contained the dining facilities. The bus then stopped at a cottage that was about one thousand feet or perhaps a city block from the dining building. One person and their luggage was dropped off and the bus continued to the next cottage, which was about five hundred feet away, and then on to the next cottage.

All of the cottages looked the same, and were positioned in an arc from the dining facilities, with all the cottages being about one thousand feet from the dining room.

Agent Jones was the eighth one to be dropped off at her cottage. Within the cottage, the main room had the usual living room furniture as well as a game table and chairs. Most inns have a recliner or two, but Agent Hope noticed that this room had none. The construction was such that it looked as if it could withstand a very severe storm. The columns were square and about a foot and a half in each direction, construction of very smooth, finished concrete. There was a porch that extended out from the house fifteen feet and completely surrounded the entire cottage. There was a bedroom and bath. Both of these were very large and modern. The interior of the cottage was paneled in what looked like mahogany. All of the nine were instructed where to find the emergency control button. There were four of these in each cottage. The sounds, and the absence of some sounds, may disturb some, so if it gets to you and for any reason you find a need for assistance, just push the button and someone from our security will join you. Mr. James also stated that the law of the island prohibits anyone from bothering anyone else, either physically or mentally.

Agent Jones checked everything, found the emergency buttons, unpacked and noticed a note on the coffee table instructing her to change into comfortable clothing and meet in the dining room for lunch as soon as she was ready. After she had dressed for the occasion, she promptly headed to the dining room.

All of the nine guests returned to the dining room within forty-five minutes of being dropped off at their cabin. All were excited about finding such attractive lodgings, and that each of the cabins appeared to be very well-constructed. Mr. James was there to greet each of the guests. He explained that the cabins were constructed to withstand very violent weather. However, he said that in the years he had been on the island, he had never seen any weather bad enough to call a storm. They were all seated and ready for lunch.

This was not what any of the nine expected. The table was prepared as you would expect in a good stateside restaurant. The meal consisted of a choice of soup or salad for appetizer, with hearty meats and vegetables for the main dish. There was no dessert. Agent Jones felt stuffed after eating her meal, and thought the islanders must be taking some kind of medication to keep them slim and trim after eating such large meals. When they were finished with lunch, Mr. James instructed the guests that they had a little time before the afternoon activities would start. He suggested that each return to their cottage to retrieve a coat and to take any prescription medicine that is required before the evening meal. He also told them that any prescriptions must be taken before nine a.m. in the morning.

Agent Jones didn't know what was in store for them, but it sounded as if it would be a busy afternoon and early evening. Agent Jones got a jacket and some knit gloves and cap from the cottage and returned to the recreational/ dining building. It appeared that this would be the center point of activities for the group.

After all of the nine had returned they boarded a van that looked more like a sightseeing bus. It had a lot of windows for viewing. They had gone about three or four miles when the van stopped beside an area that was enclosed with a cyclone fence that was probably eight to ten feet high. Mr. James proceeded to explain what they saw: this was one of the locations where some tests were being conducted under direction of one of the major medical schools in the U.S. They were not at liberty to reveal which medical schools.

James proceeded on his brief tour, "This area is a peninsula and is completely fenced off from the rest of the island. Briefly, I will mention that it is the site of one study being conducted, and that there are ten subjects that have various types of non-contagious diseases. All have been classified as terminal. They have come here from the U.S. as part of their treatment plans, and will be here for a two-year period. They will eat the same food as do the residents of this island. As each is able, they will be kept in activity. So far, the group has been here seven months and all members are still alive and appear to be in better health than when they arrived here. If this study's successful, another study will be conducted to determine which of the individual aspects helped the medical problem. Was it the absence of technology? Was it something about the food? Or the abundant amount of rest?

"Throughout this study, reports are sent to the school conducting the study detailing the condition of each participant on a monthly basis. All of the activity behind this fence is about five miles down the road. This is a secured area. Now we will continue on to our destination."

They drove for another ten or fifteen minutes and stopped in front of another well-constructed building. Inside were water fountains and restrooms for the group. In the background were foothills. After the necessary bathroom break, the group was told that they were going to hike to the next point, which would be three miles over the foothills. Mr. James reassured the group that there was no danger. The trail was easy walking and they would not encounter any wild animals or strangers along the way.

They started out and were surprised how easy it was to walk in the area. The trail was something like a walking trail you would expect to see in some of the big cities in the United States. The climate was great which made the walking easy.

Thirty minutes into the walk another building came into view. As they approached, it was evident that this building was the same type as the one they had just left. As they arrived, Mr. James informed them that they would be at this rest stop for as long as a half hour. He said that he wanted to show something to the group after they had an opportunity to use the restroom and get water. All of the group were really aware that a candy or nut or drink machine was not located at this rest stop, as you would find at most rest stops in the states. The quality of the building at the rest stop was superior to anything you would expect to find on a remote island in the Pacific. The construction looked as if it would last at least a hundred years, and to have just been cleaned.

After the break, Mr. James said that he wanted to remind each of the group that we could eat any of the fruit found on the island. That is, all except one, and it could be eaten at certain times. He showed us several trees in the area and made sure to point out the "Rainbow trees."

"As you will notice, some of the fruit on these trees is green, some white, and some orange. Due to our unique climate, these trees will have ripe fruit on some, and others will be budding and also have ripening fruit. So it is possible to get ripe fruit at almost any time. It has already been explained to each of you that this fruit starts out as green. As it ripens it changes to white. When ripe and edible it is orange. Remember, the fruit cannot be eaten unless it is orange. When it is green-colored, the skin is tough, about like trying to peel a pecan. When it turns white, its skin or peel becomes soft, and the pulp and juice are white also. One bite of white fruit, or just two drops of white juice, will kill you in twenty-four hours. Before it is ripe, the pulp and the juice have no taste. The juice is as clear as water. You will not get sick or feel any effects of tasting this unripen fruit. You will just die and your body will be disposed of, and there will be no record of you having been here on this island." He cut several of the Rainbow Fruit balls and said that he would eat some to show the group that they were okay to eat, since they were orange and did not have any white showing. Most of the group was nervous, but after tasting, all wanted more. This was really great tasting fruit.

After all had tasted, and more water and trips to the restroom, the group started out on the trail. It appeared that the group took about forty minutes to cover a mile on the trail. They soon came to another rest stop, and it appeared that the distance was a little over a mile. As they entered the rest area, they observed a motorized rail car with a coach attached on the backside. The group thought that this reminded them of the type of rail car that was referred to as a cog train that was used to go up to the top of Pike's Peak, back in the States. They could see steep hills, not mountains, in the background. Mr. James explained that the group would have another rest room break, and then board the cog train for a trip to the top of the hill.

After boarding the train, everyone agreed that it was surprising to find something as modern as this cog train in a remote island in the Pacific. Of course, when you think about the great way everything else has been constructed on this island, it made sense that the cog train would also be excellent.

The trip to the top of the hill was slow, and on reaching the top, there appeared to be a building similar to the one that was constructed in the dining room where the group had lunch. This had to be the high point on the island. The view was great. Mr. James informed the group that the trail leading from the building would lead to a geyser much like Old Faithful. Everyone wanted to see the geyser.

He said it was safe to go and observe, but they should not get off the walkway and observation deck.

Return back to this location in one hour. Then, please clean up and prepare for our evening meal, which we will be having at this location."

Everything at this site was first-class. Of course it should be, considering what each of the group was paying for the week.

Upon reaching the geyser area they all agreed that the view reminded them of seeing Old Faithful back in the States. They got to see the geyser spew, and returned back to the location where they would have their evening meal.

All were enjoying the view when they were informed that the evening meal was ready to be served. The staff at this location for the evening meal seemed to be a little more relaxed and more casual. This could be because Upchurch was not present. Upchurch did not appear to be unkind. It seemed that all liked him even though he ruled with an iron hand. Everyone thought that he was fair when dealing with problems.

The entire group was amazed at the quality, and especially the quantity, of food that had been prepared for them. The chef must have thought the group consisted of construction workers due to the large amount of food he prepared. Jones said it was an odd feeling, being in this remote and small island in the Pacific, and all dressed in hiking clothes, and eating the food you would expect to find in an upper-class restaurant. It was odd, but didn't bother any of the group.

Everyone greatly enjoyed the fine meal. Afterwards, they walked around in the restaurant area and enjoyed the view. Then they boarded the cog train for the trip back down the hill. It was beginning to get dark and the lights were on in the rest area and those that led to another down the trail.

After exiting the cog train, the group looked around a bit before entering the trail to the next rest stop, which was about a mile. They took the necessary rest room break at the stop and then started down a well-lit trail towards the next rest stop. Before long they arrived at the rest stop where the van was waiting to return them to the recreational area. None of the group wanted to stay around the rest area. Everyone expressed that it had been a great day, but each was ready for a bath and bed. They must have been tired and didn't realize that it was not quite nine p.m.

Agent Jones felt that she would have a difficult time sleeping because it was extremely quiet and she was accustomed to hearing all types of noise during the night—mainly, emergency vehicles making emergency runs, garbage trucks, and delivery vans on their daily route. In spite of the lack of customary noise, Agent Jones had a great night's rest.

The next morning she was ready for some breakfast, and looking forward to the day's events on the second day of her visit to the island.

Before leaving the recreational area, Mr. James told each of the guests that there was an alarm in each of the cabins that would be activated from the recreation building at seven a.m. each day. It would continue to ring until the occupant of the cabin operates a shut-off button located in such a place that would make it necessary to get out of bed to turn off the alarm. By manually shutting off the alarm, the staff would know that everyone was awake and on the move. Breakfast is served at 8:30 sharp, so this should give everyone ample time to wake up and get ready. If someone was missing and had not arrived at the recreation room by 9:30, the staff would go to the cabin for a wellness check. Whatever the outcome, the rest of the activities for the day will start at ten a.m.

Agent Jones had been awake for some time when the alarm sounded at seven a.m. She and some of the group got to the dining room before the designated 8:30 serving time. Everyone was attempting to guess the type of activity that would be on the schedule for the second day of their visit.

Breakfast consisted of coffee, juice, choice of bacon, sausage, or ham, and eggs cooked as desired. There was no syrup, jelly, or honey.

During their inspection when they arrived on the island, each had been asked to step on the weighing scales. This number had been recorded, and they were told that this procedure would be repeated as they departed the island. Agent Jones thought if they were to continue to be fed like construction workers, she would not be surprised if she would be twenty pounds heavier on Saturday morning when they leave for the trip back to Noumea.

After breakfast, Mr. James informed the group that it was Tuesday, the second day of their stay on the island. He said that they would be leaving this area at ten a.m. and they should return to their cottage to get any clothes, medicine, or anything else that they might need until nine p.m. Wednesday. They would be sleeping elsewhere that night.

The group returned to the recreation area a few minutes before ten a.m. The driver of the van was ready, and they left the area. They did not have any idea what they were going to be doing that day.

The driver did not appear to be in any hurry. After about forty minutes, the van stopped at what appeared to be a nice farmhouse. Of the nine guests that were left after the one lady had been escorted off the island for not complying with the rules, four were female and five were male. Two of the females were dropped off at the farmhouse. A female employee was waiting to greet them and successively escorted them into the house. Agent Jones and another female guest were dropped off at the next farmhouse. This house appeared to be just like the first farmhouse, and it was less than a quarter of a mile down the road. The house and outbuildings appeared to be of very sound construction, just like everything else on the island.

The men continued on, with three dropped off at a farmhouse, and two at the next. Agent Jones and the other female guest, Wilma, were escorted into the house by the employee, the farmer's wife. Agent Jones was amazed at the size of this woman. She looked as if she could have been a dancing partner with Fred Astaire in some of his movies back in the sixties. Every person who lived on this island looked to be in perfect health. Agent Jones thought that when she first saw these islanders, that they were all sick. The fact was that she just wasn't accustomed to seeing anyone who wasn't overweight. Now that she had seen many like this, she realized that these islanders were the really healthy ones.

The farmer's wife was named Carol, and she acted as if she was really glad to meet Agent Jones and Wilma. Carol said that her husband, son, and a couple of the neighbor's sons would be in from the fields shortly. They would all have a noon meal together. Carol had prepared a beef stew and cornbread for the lunch. Wilma saw the amount of food that had been prepared and said it looked as if enough to feed a dozen hard-working people.

The men came in, were introduced, and shortly began eating their noon meal. Agent Jones thought that the stew was the best she had ever had.

After the meal, the men went back to the field and the females cleaned the kitchen. Carol revealed the next part of the day's agenda, which was that they were going to the tomato field to do some planting. She went on to explain that in the beginning of this island development they had different activities from the guests. It seemed that most of the guests were mainly interested in getting their body in shape to look like all the people on the island. Carol explained that one of the universities that were conducting an experiment had wanted Upchurch to develop a community like this island in the United States. Upchurch laughed at the idea. He said that it would be impossible to be located in an area that could be completely isolated from the rest of the population of the United States. Also, it would not be legal to give Upchurch the authority that he had on this island. They offered him a great sum of money to attempt to make this work in the U.S. He just laughed at the offer because he had all the money that he could ever spend in his lifetime.

Carol took them out to the tomato field. She explained that there were three areas. There was one area where the tomatoes were ripe and being picked. The second area was where new growth was forming. The third area was where the three of them were going to be planting new tomato plants. She explained that this was possible to have new plants and mature producing plants at the same time all year long due to their climate.

Carol then relayed the arrangements the islanders have with Upchurch, "While we live on the island we all have duties to perform. In exchange, everything is provided for us. All of us are free to leave at any time we wish. After the age of 18, if we desire to leave we would be paid one thousand dollars for each month we worked on the island. If we leave before the age of thirty-eight, there is no possibility of returning. However; we can leave after the age of twenty-five for a two-week's vacation, a check for five thousand dollars, and then return. We have the option to do this every two years. If we stay until the age of thirty-eight and wish to leave, Mr. Upchurch will pay for medical insurance and give us four times what the maximum Social Security is at that time in the States. You would think that was a very tempting deal to take, but only two people have elected to leave after the age of thirty-eight." Carol went on to say that they had a very pleasant life here on the island.

Carol showed Agent Jones and Wilma how to set out the tomato plants. They got a lot accomplished and it became late in the day. Carol said they would have to go in a little early so they could get cleaned up for the evening activities. There would be a pot-luck supper at the community house and then a prayer meeting. There was a community house on the island that was convenient for eight to ten families. After they went into the house and bathed and dressed, Carol had both of them help her with the food that she was taking to the potluck supper: stuffed bell peppers, and there were a lot of them.

Agent Jones still could not understand how these people could eat so much and still look so neat and trim. No person on the island was overweight. That is, no person that lived on the island. Visitors were another story.

Carol asked Agent Jones and Wilma if they noticed that very few islanders wore glasses. They said they had not, but now that she mentioned it there were only a few that wore glasses. Carol explained, "Everyone on the island eats a lot of tomatoes, and there seemed to be something in the tomatoes that made for healthy eyes. For that, I am glad my family farms the tomatoes."

Also, nearly all of the families here served gazpacho several times a week. Carol said that hers had a lot of tomatoes along with cucumbers, green bell peppers, red bell peppers, zucchini, and onions. Along with the vegetables they added juice from carrots, celery, beets, and parsley. They also added a little vinegar and olive oil, and a small amount of hot sauce. This was just one of the ways that they got their daily vegetable, since gazpacho is a soup that is served cold and is easily made and was able to keep for a few days.

When they were ready to go to the community house, Agent Jones was curious about how they would get all the stuffed bell peppers to the community house. It turned out to be simple: they had a little wagon, something like Americans would use in a flower garden. This was a small pull-along, with four wheels and side-boards. The whole thing could not have been longer than two or two-and-a-half feet. It was easy to pull, so they got the food to the community house with little effort.

Each of the farmers that attended the dinner also had a wagon. This was like the pioneer days of America, when the pioneers would gather for social and prayer meetings. They would have their horse and buggy outside the meeting place. At this place, each family would have their wagon outside. This plan seemed to work pretty well. All the ones gathered here at this community house lived about a quarter of a mile from this location. This was a weekly gathering, and all seemed to be very happy sharing this time and meal with others. They made all the guests feel comfortable, and accepted them just like they were part of the group.

After visiting for a while, they had a meal that consisted of food that each family had brought. Agent Jones and Wilma were hungry, and each ate more than usual. Jones thought that if she continued to eat like this for the rest of the week, she would definitely gain the previously projected 20 pounds by the end of her stay on the island. She thought about this and realized that the eating habits of the islanders were very different from what was the custom in the United States. These islanders did not have a break for coffee and donuts in the morning, and did not have any kind of snack in the afternoon. Also, Agent Jones realized that although this was just the end of the second day of her visit, she had not seen any desserts.

After the meal, the group took seats and had a short prayer meeting. Nothing mentioned indicated any particular denomination. Some offered prayer for thanksgiving and prayed for the health and wellbeing of the guests.

It was not a typical prayer meeting. These folks were mainly talking about what a great day this had been, and how they had enjoyed their time spent with the guests. They thanked God for their many blessings and for their life on this island. They said there would be a short church service the following day as well.

By the time Jones and Wilma got back to the farm, they were both ready for a good night's sleep. Agent Jones was thinking about the next day and what her schedule would be.

Upon awakening the next morning, Agent Jones felt so great after all the activity the previous day. As she walked into the eating area, she observed that Carol, Carol's husband and son, and Wilma were already gathered at the table and breakfast was about to be served.

After a prayer of thanksgiving, the group started to eat. Agent Jones thought the amount of food at the table would be enough to feed at least eight or ten people instead of the five that were there.

After their meal, Carol, Jones, and Wilma cleared the kitchen while Carol told them what the activity would be for the day. They were going to be canning green beans with potatoes, pickled beets, pickled asparagus, and believe it or not, eggs. Several families on this island did this once or twice a week. Because of the unique climate of the island, they could do this all year, since it was possible to continue planting during the harvesting season. These products were transported to their retail outlet in Noumea. The citizens of Noumea were thrilled to purchase these items. All the money from sales went to charity in Noumea and in the United States.

"Last year one of the weekly guests was the owner of a very large health food store in the U.S. He was impressed with the products and asked if he could be purchase an order at wholesale and have them shipped to his store. We took him up on his offer and sold each of the jarred items for the equivalent to two dollars each in American money. We did ask that he cover the shipping fees. He wanted all that we could send to him. That was when we changed from canning the products one day a week to twice a week as we do now. These stay on the shelves in the Noumea store for thirty days before they are sold. They had different size and shape jars for each one which they thought justified the same price for each. The beets and eggs were used in the same size jar." Carol told them.

Wilma had never seen anyone canning anything. Jones had seen her grandmother make jelly from grapes and peaches. Carol showed them how to properly place the fresh produce into the appropriately sized jars.

They took a break for lunch. One of the items included in their lunch was pickled asparagus. Agent Jones, though typically not a fan of asparagus, thought it was much better than any she had ever eaten. She enjoyed every bite of it. It was very clear why the man from the health food store wanted this product in his store.

They continued pickling until late in the afternoon. Carol was very efficient and was able to prepare the evening meal while still directing the two guests in the process of canning. This meal was much like all that had been available since Agent Jones had been on the island. There was a large amount of food and, again, no desserts.

After dinner and cleaning the kitchen, they all went to the community center. This was different from the day before. When they were there on Tuesday, it seemed that the gathering was mainly a time for eating and sharing the recent events of their lives. This day, the meal had been consumed before they arrived at the community center, so there was some visiting and then a couple of songs, a prayer meeting, and then everyone headed back to their homes. There was time for Jones and Wilma to return to the cottage they had first been assigned, close to the recreational room. When they returned to their cabin, they immediately hit the shower and went bed. Neither woman had any idea what kind of an activity they would find themselves involved in on Thursday.

When Agent Jones arrived at the dining room on Thursday morning, she was yet again surprised at the bountiful amount of food that had been prepared for so few people. She remembered that each of the nine guests had been weighed when they arrived on Monday. They were also told that they would also be weighed when they were ready to depart the island on Saturday. It seemed to Agent Jones that her first estimate of weight gain had not been enough.

After breakfast, Mr. James notified the group that they would have time to go back to their cottage to change into clothes appropriate for horseback riding and grab any medicine they would need at any time until nine p.m. tomorrow, which would be Friday. They would need to meet back at the recreational hall at ten o'clock to board a van headed for the ranch area. They would be sleeping outside under the stars and sleeping bags would be provided at the ranch.

It didn't take Agent Jones long to complete her breakfast routine, take any medicine that she needed, and dress for the trip to the ranch. When she got back to the community center, about half the group were already there, and all were excited about going to the ranch.

Well, all were excited except two of the more "city slicker" guests who had never been really close to nature. They were a little nervous and didn't know what to expect.

The group boarded the van and was in the hill country within just a few minutes of travel. Jones felt the scenery was easily the most beautiful she ever remembered seeing in all of her travels. She was thinking that Hollywood moviemakers would be thrilled to have the opportunity to produce a movie in this area.

When they arrived at the ranch, they saw a very large headquarters building, several smaller buildings, a couple of big barns, and several cottages like the ones they had been assigned back on the island's center of operations. They were greeted by Guy Duke, who was the ranch manager. After they had all assembled in the central meeting room, Duke explained what they would be doing for the rest of the day and what to expect for Friday. They were told to assemble back at the central location by eleven-thirty wearing jeans, boots, hat, and a light jacket. Until then they were free to walk around the area and check out anything that looked interesting to them. He explained they would be going up into the hills to round up cattle that they would drive or head back to this area. He said this would be a night to remember, since they would be sleeping out among the stars.

After their lunch, each of the nine was assigned a horse, and the stirrup length of the saddle was adjusted to fit comfort. After a brief walk around riding the horse, they all felt comfortable and started following Duke. The route they were taking was mainly an upward trail. After about one hour on the trail, they approached a rest stop. The rest stop seemed out of place in the middle of nowhere as it was surprisingly modern. Much similar to what you would expect to find in a rest area on the highway in the United States. Just like everything else, this facility was constructed as if it would last a hundred or more years. After the restroom break, the group started out again, and along the trail they met two cowboys that were rounding up stray cattle.

Four of the group joined the cowboys while the rest continued upward on the trail with Guy Duke. They encountered some stray cattle, and after instructions from Duke they drove the strays in front of the others until they came to some cattle pens. It was a great experience. Some in the group had never been on horseback prior to this trip. Some even said it was one of the most enjoyable days of their life. Just wait until they see how sore they would be from several hours in the saddle!

At the area where the cattle were herded into holding pens, they observed some cabins similar to what they had at the central area. It was amazing how this had all been planned for the comfort of the guests. Four of the cowboys took control of the horses after they had corralled the cattle. They were assigned cabins and told they should come back to this area after a thirty minute break and be ready to go up into the hills. Duke explained that the cabins that had been assigned to them would be for sleeping Friday night.

Len Hankins was the cowboy in charge of the next segment of their day's journey. They left the area and were still going upward to an area where they would locate the cattle they were to bring back to this area. Along the way they observed several strays. Hankins said they would not bother with them now but would include them with the herd as they came back out of the hills tomorrow. After more time in the saddle, they came to an open area where they saw another of the modern rest areas. There was also a chuck wagon in the area. The campfire was burning and when they got off the horses they were told that campfire coffee was ready for them.

The cowboys took charge of the guests' horses. Most of the group had never heard of campfire coffee. After they had a cup of coffee in their hands, they heard an explanation as to how the coffee was made in a tin can. It was getting pretty cool and all agreed that this was the very best coffee they had ever had. Needless to say, if the coffee had been served to them in a stateside restaurant, none of them would have thought it was worth drinking. Agent Jones had been enjoying the activities and really didn't realize that it was approaching time for an evening meal, when they were told to assemble back at the campfire, after a restroom break.

Afterwards, Agent Jones and Wilma were some of the first guests assembled at the campfire. The view from there was something you would expect to see on a travel brochure. Hankins told the group that this meal would be a little different from what the early pioneers of the American West would have had. Whereas the meat they were about to eat was prepared much earlier, the pioneers would have only been able to eat right after the animal was slaughtered; the rest of the meat would have been wither smoked, dried, or left to spoil while they were on a trail. They all had more campfire coffee, enjoyed the view, looked at the fire, and heard some tales of the early years on this island.

Soon the meal was ready. The cook mixed up some type of sauce that he brushed on the slab of brisket while it was cooking. The meal was simple and consisted solely of meat, beans, and bread (or "hardtack," as the cowboys referred to it). However, the meal was different than the typical meat, beans and bread Jones was accustomed to. The meal was fantastic and after some more tales of the early days it was time to get some rest. Sleeping bags were dispersed for everyone.

They were told that nothing would bother them while they slept; they had no reason to be nervous about any wild animals. After a while, the sounds of nature were very soothing and everyone received a good night sleep under the stars.

Wilma was the first guest up the next morning. The campfire was still going strong and the coffee was ready. After breakfast, the group saddled up and was ready for what the cowboys called a "roundup." They were going to drive the cattle from the upper range down to their ranch headquarters.

The group came upon a group of about 200 cows grazing. Agent Jones thought it looked like a big job for nine greenhorns and four cowboys. Everything seemed to be going without any problem. They soon came upon a chuck wagon at a different location.

The cook had coffee ready and a camp stew prepared for their noon meal. A cowboy and three of the nine guests stayed with the cattle to keep them from straying while the others ate. Then they were relieved so they could eat their noon meal. Afterwards, they continued down from the high country.

Agent Jones was glad when she saw the headquarters building coming into view. She was ready to get out of the saddle.

The cattle were pinned in the corral without much trouble. The cowboys took charge of the horses that the nine guests had been riding, and the guests returned to the assigned cabins to do the necessary things to prepare to assemble in the dining room for the evening meal.

Duke and Hankins were both waiting in the dining hall when Jones, Wilma, and the rest of the guests arrived. Anytime the nine guests were assembled and waiting for instructions or waiting for a meal to be served, or just had an opportunity to talk with any of the islanders, they had plenty of questions. The question that most of them asked was, "How do you islanders stay so thin and healthy looking?" The answers were always the same. All of them said they ate as much food as they wanted but no desserts and no junk food. Also, they got plenty of exercise, maybe too much at times. And there were no drugs or alcohol on the island. They were all pleased with the arrangement and none of them ever thought about going on a diet. After the last of the nine guests arrived at the dining room, Duke got their attention and told them that since this would be their last evening meal on the island, "It is scheduled to be a meal that will remain forever with you." He said that the meal would consist of a small dinner salad, steamed vegetables, and a resin baked potato.

"There will be ample sour cream and butter with the potatoes. The meat will be your choice of prime rib or filet of beef. The prime rib has been cooking for several days, and the filet will be cooked to your liking. Both of the meats will be something you will want to tell your grandchildren in your golden years. Are any of you familiar with a potato being cooked in resin? The potatoes are washed and patted dry and placed in hot resin. When cooked to perfection, they will float to the top of the resin. They are removed and wrapped in a paper similar to a grocery bag. The resin sticks to the paper and after a few minutes the potato can be slit open. Then you may add sour cream and/or butter. Besides the canned vegetables that we sell at our Noumea store, we also package and quick-freeze some of the choice cuts of beef. We sell and ship these to a restaurant in New York. The remaining beef is packaged for ribs, roast, and some ground beef. We also quick-freeze these and sell and ship to a market in San Francisco and Dallas in the United States.

"Enough of this talk. I know all of you are ready for food, so let's proceed with our evening meal." Duke gestured towards the buffet.

There was very little talking during the meal. After the meal and some small talk, the group of guests retired to their cabin. It had been a busy day and all were ready for a shower and bed.

When they arrived at the recreational room on Saturday morning, all seemed to be quieter than usual. Perhaps many of the thoughts were on the past week's activity. Agent Jones agreed with some of the others that this had not been anything like they had expected. Really, none had known what to expect, but they sure didn't expect anything close to what they had seen in these few days.

After breakfast, Upchurch and James were present to meet with the group before they departed for the short trip back to Noumea. Mr. Upchurch reminded them of the healthy food they had eaten this week.

"I'm sure many of you feel that you have gained a lot of weight during your stay here. The food has been delicious and plentiful. As you recall, all of you were weighed when you first came to the island on Monday. You will be weighed again here shortly. Also, remember before you depart from this island, your luggage will be inspected to make certain that no fruit or vegetable be removed from this island. The only time this can be done is in a planned operation such as the islanders do when they export the meat and canned goods."

Agent Jones felt certain that she had gained twenty pounds eating all the great meals. When she weighed in, she was surprised to learn that she had actually *lost* nine pounds! The rest of the group had the same type of results.

After the weight check and luggage inspection, they all boarded for their return trip to Noumea.

TWELVE

Norris was at the dock area when Agent Jones came ashore in Noumea. They immediately headed for a coffee shop so they could sit down and discuss the events of the past week. It struck Jones as odd that she would be sitting and drinking coffee, opposed to the past week where there was much activity while drinking coffee.

The first question that Norris asked was, "Did you locate the poison?"

Agent Jones's reply was, "Yes. I am most positive that I did. Let me tell you how unusual it is."

She told him all about the Rainbow Ball, and how it would be hard to get any of it off of the island. There must be a way; after all, Price had found some way to get the poison off the island. "Upchurch and the staff made it pretty clear that anyone caught trying to remove any of the poison would be killed right there and the body would be disposed of and there would be no record showing that person had ever been on Bonita Island."

She then related to Norris what had happened to the lady that was removed from the island upon inspection at their arrival at the island. Trying to find out how Price smuggled the poison off the island and back to the U.S. without getting caught was going to be a problem.

In the States, Agent Hope and I had so much success with the entrapment of illegal aliens that slipped past the border at Laredo that we were asked to go to the crossing at

El Paso. The Border Patrol felt that we would be a big help to them at that location.

It wasn't long after we arrived at the checkpoint in El Paso that twenty percent more illegal persons were turned back daily. We were utilizing the method of the GTDs attached to the various suspects' cars where they would later be apprehended at various points along their route. A lot of the illegal activity had been stopped, but there still was a lot to be done to stop both people and drugs from entering the U.S. illegally from Mexico.

One member of the Border Patrol told Hope the office in San Diego would like the same sort of help.

The Mexican government had refused to help with the drug problem. Anytime a drug shipment got past the border check point and reached its destination, the money earned through its sell would be returned to Mexico. Also, a large percentage of people that snuck past the U.S. checkpoints were mostly of the unemployed Mexican population. So, by standing by and not helping the U.S. with this problem, they were able to increase revenue in Mexico and make unemployment rates better there.

The trip from Noumea back to the U.S. was relatively uneventful. However, Agent Jones did get a little upset at a lady across the aisle from her that had an ample supply of bubble gum. She made a lot of noise while chewing, and then she was an expert at blowing large bubbles and popping the gum. Norris was able to have a good nap while this was going on. Finally, the lady got tired, spit out her gum and took a nap. A relieved Jones took advantage of the quiet. She immediately closed her eyes, and drifted off to some much needed sleep.

When Norris and Jones got to the office in Irving, Small and Watson were there and anxious to hear the details of their trip to Noumea and the Bonita Island. Agent Jones wasted no time relating to the others information about the poison that was used to kill the insured subjects from the Henry cases. She told them about the great looking, physically fit people that lived on Bonita Island. After they had talked for some time, Norris suggested that they contact Hope and me to request our return from El Paso, where we were posted working with the Border Patrol.

The project that we would now be working on (trying to discover how Price and his associates have been able to sneak the poisonous Rainbow Ball juice off Bonita Island) should be classified as "Top Secret."

The agents discussed what would happen if and when they were able to stop these people from removing poison from the island. Also, what would happen if one of the six government agents went undercover and tried to smuggle the poison off of the island?

The Baker's Dozen has a code number to call a meeting without going into detail as to what its purpose is. The code was 183, always followed by a statement that the person contacted needed to come to a certain office to fill in the information on a new Form 183. Hope and I were contacted and notified to come to the office in Irving to complete new Forms 183.

When we arrived at the Irving office, we were briefed about the results from the trip to the island of Bonita. After some discussions about how this poison had been removed from the island, Jones suggested that we each make some notes indicating possible smuggling methods the mafia members might be using. Agent Jones said she felt certain that if it was determined that if anyone was trying to export poison from the island, they would be eliminated immediately. Upchurch made it very clear that his rules would be observed or there would be severe consequences. Hope told the rest of the agents about the lady who had tried to take prohibited items to the island.

We continued brainstorming for two days trying to find a plausible solution. Norris suggested we page the Admiral Baker with the 183 code. Within a few days, Baker arrived in Irving, and reiterated to the group that this was indeed a top secret investigation.

"Where are we on the investigation right now?" Baker asked.

Agent Jones told him, "We have been trying to figure out how Price and his buddies are smuggling the poison from the island. We all brainstormed possible theories and wrote down our ideas. We have kept our notes in locked, secure locations while away from the office, and we plan to destroy all of them after this discussion has been completed."

Norris continued, "We combed through the ideas brought forth. All but two, have been eliminated."

"Let's hear them," commanded Baker.

"I was thinking that since prescription medication was permitted on the island, perhaps a prescription bottle containing liquid such as eye drops could have be emptied on the island, and then refilled with poison." Norris suggested.

Watson cleared her throat. "Along the same lines, I thought possibly an ink fountain pen was brought to the island, with its ink replaced with poison. Like prescriptions, pens were not included on the list of items prohibited on the island. Therefore, Price and his associates could have used either as a vessel for the poison, and would have thus avoided detection from Upchurch and staff."

After another couple of hours of back and forth discussion, Baker told the group he needed to place a call to one or two officials in Washington to summon a Special Forces group. He instructed the Baker's Dozen to make necessary contacts with the authorities in some select states in the Northeast and Southwest to retrieve the top four criminals in each state known to be involved in the drug trade. The names on the list would also need to be those with a known connection to the mafia. These crooks were going to be ones guilty beyond a shadow of a doubt, but that authorities had been unable to convict due to a lack of admissible information or because of legal maneuvers.

Baker said he would be in contact with the group in Irving after he meets with the contacts in Washington and after a plan is devised to get the poison off the island of Bonita. Baker left after that and the group at the Irving office left for the day.

I was the first one in the office the next morning, and took the initiative to spread a map of the U.S. on the conference table. Once everyone arrived and had a cup of coffee, it was decided that we would concentrate on three states in each region of interest. In the Northeast, we would focus on New Jersey, Connecticut, and New York. In the Southwest we would focus on Arizona, Nevada, and California. We knew it would be impossible to obtain the information that we needed by phone, so we made plans to make personal visits to necessary contacts in each of the selected states. Once the lists were produced from the contacts, we would need to visit the district attorneys in the most crime-infested cities in each of the selected states to have them confine the list to just two from the largest city, and one each from two more cities in each state.

Our cover was to say that the federal government wants to make a study of all the people who were breaking the law and yet able to avoid conviction. In many cases, although authorities knew they were involved in crime—mainly the drug trade—evidence could not be obtained to convict them of a crime. Some of these were well known to be head of a certain group of people dealing in drugs or prostitution and authorities could not even get enough solid evidence to make an arrest.

We decided how we would split up the six selected states. As usual, we would go in pairs. Small and Watson would take California and Nevada; Norris and Jones would make the contacts in New York and New Jersey; Hope and I would take on Arizona and Connecticut.

THIRTEEN

When Admiral Baker arrived in Washington, he wasted no time working on the poison problem. He met up with two of his most trusted associates. These were men who had been tried and tested over the years, and had been trusted with very secret information many times. Baker assured them that what he was going to discuss with them was top secret. He told them about the Henry cases, and how agents had been determining the source of the poison used to kill the subjects without leaving an obvious cause of death. The agents had determined the poison was being smuggled off a small island in the Pacific Ocean by Justin Price, a known affiliate of the mafia. The island, Bonita, is privately-owned and is not a possession of any country; therefore it is self-governed by the owner, Chester Upchurch.

"There is much reason to believe that if Upchurch were to find anyone trying to remove poison from the island, they would be put to death. Our agents say that Upchurch is fair in dealing with people that live on the island. Our agents say that if Upchurch found Price in possession of poison, that there would not be any trial. He would be put to death, and there would not be any record of Price ever being on the island. So, Price has taken great measures to sneak the poison off the island, and we need to know exactly what these measures are."

Baker mentioned the two ideas brought up by the other agents (the medicine bottles and pen ideas), and then the men dived into a discussion of the other alternative ways the agents could try to get poison off the island. Many ideas were put forth and then scrapped. One mentionable idea was that perhaps Price and his men could make a quick assault on the island with helicopters. This was later decided as no good. Any plan that obvious would certainly result in death if the agent if he was caught. After wracking their brains for a few hours, Baker and the men did not have a concrete plan, but Baker had an idea that he kept to himself.

Baker made a decision to contact someone else and the Secretary of Defense to ask for assistance. Of course, Baker didn't say who it was he was going to talk to, but the two men knew that Baker reported directly to the President of the United States. They felt safe in their assumption as to whom he was going to talk with before he approached the Secretary of Defense.

Baker was not one to hesitate about action once he has made a decision. He called a telephone number that he and a few select others had known. When the phone was answered, Baker gave the code number to designate that he had authority to ask for appointment time with the President. He was told to be in the Oval Office at three p.m. on the next day. This suited Baker because he had already planned what he would discuss with the President. He went to bed feeling confident that the plan he had devised would work to accomplish his goal.

He awoke the next morning and went over once in his mind just how the plan should work. He felt confident when he arrived at the Oval Office just before three p.m. He was admitted, seated in the Oval Office, and offered coffee just before the President entered the room.

Knowing the President's time was very valuable, Baker got right to the point. Before he revealed his plan, he briefed the President on all the events that had unfolded. He concluded that the unknown causes of death in the Henry cases have been caused by a Rainbow Ball that is only found on one island and is being transported to the U.S. via Justin Price, a person of interest affiliated with the mafia.

"Bonita Island is not a possession of any country and is privately owned and ruled with an iron hand, and at the same time the owner is very reasonable. There are no jails on the island, and justice is swift. One of our agents recently spent a week there and reported that death would be the punishment for any person removing poison from the island if they were caught." Baker reported. "Mr. President, if possible, I would like to work with the Secretary of Defense. The plan I have devised involves cooperating with the owner of the island, Chester Upchurch, to devise an arrangement where he could help us eliminate some of our most undesirable criminals. Of course, in exchange this would remain a very secret project and we would consider his island to be a 'favored nation.' I am most positive Upchurch will lend an assisting hand to us as this mission would illuminate the method Price is using to smuggle poison off his island."

The President agreed. "I will personally notify the Secretary of Defense of his assignment to be at your disposal. Feel free to contact him at your earliest convenience." The President then concluded, as he usually did, "We did not have this conversation."

Baker knew that the Secretary of Defense was going to be very busy the next few days, so Baker would contact him later. In the meantime, he got in touch with two of the supervisors from the Special Forces group. He set up a meeting with them for ten a.m. the next day. The meeting was to take place at a location where they had met many times in the past to discuss very important and confidential information. This location was checked daily to be certain that no surveillance or bugs had been placed where conversations could be monitored. Baker met with them at ten the next morning and informed both of them about the case that he wanted them to help finalize. He started with the information about the insurance cases where the causes of death could not be determined, briefly what had been involved in the investigation, and finally how they had located what was used to cause these deaths where autopsy did not reveal any reason for death.

Now, the following is the reason he needs help from the Special Forces. All of the agents under their supervision have received special training and all are aware that they are an elite group that can be called upon at any time to eliminate an enemy of the U.S. Baker told them that he wanted to be in a position to administer this unknown poison to known mafia and drug dealers when we are able to obtain the poison. We are trying to formalize a plan where we can get enough poison to eliminate twenty-four people who are known to be involved in drugs and mafia activity but cannot be convicted because of some loophole in the law or because they have some pretty sly lawyers.

"These agents will need to get into position so they will be able to administer just two drops of the poison to the intended victim. Your agents could plan to get close to the victim by getting into their group, by being a waiter at their favorite hangout, or any way you can devise. We want to set this up so this can be done about six months from now. All would have to be done within a two-day period, that is, this poison would have to be administered during the two-day period, and June the first and second would be a good time. This would give our other contacts time to work out a plan to obtain this poison. We feel that we would be able to get enough poison to eliminate the twenty-four that we have discussed."

Baker told them that this effort could be wasted if they were unable to obtain the poison, but he felt certain that the plan he had would be workable. Baker informed these two that he would have a list of the names of the twenty-four people that needed to be removed from this earth. This list should be ready in two to three days. But you can go ahead and begin selecting your agents for this project. After you get these names and their cities of operations, and get your agents in place, get back in touch with me. You each know the code number to give my operator so I can be contacted. Also, they would need a plan where the agents could be supplied with the poison prior to June the first. Baker left the meeting and was thinking about the meeting he would have with the Secretary of Defense. Both Baker and the Secretary of Defense had scheduled meetings that would prevent them from getting together during the next two days. So they planned to meet on Monday in the office of the Secretary of Defense.

As usual, Baker was on time for the meeting on Monday. They got right down to business and Baker informed him all about the case that the agents were trying to solve. After a lot of discussion about how to get the poison, it was agreed that they would treat the owner of the island of Bonita just as if he were the head of an independent nation. Both men felt that there was no other way to accomplish their goal.

The plan would be to send a message to Chester Upchurch and request that he receive two visitors from the U.S. These visitors would be the Secretary of Defense and Admiral Baker. The message would list four dates and times in the month of January. Upchurch would select a date and these two visitors to the island would arrive on a carrier that would be off the coast of the island on the selected date. These two visitors would then transfer to a destroyer escort and, with permission from Chester Upchurch, would tie up at the island dock and remain there until the visit would be concluded. Both agreed that this was a workable plan and they would proceed as outlined.

However, Baker also wanted to obtain a complete list of the twenty-four that the D.A.s in the six selected states most wanted to be eliminated.

Baker left the meeting and was anxious to get in touch with the group. No one answered when Baker called the office in Irving. This wasn't too unusual since that office was used as a field office for agents on cases in the general area. After getting no answer from that office, Baker contacted me by phone. The progress report from Agent Hope and me was good. We had completed the contact with district attorney in Hartford, Connecticut. The D.A. had been very helpful. He said that it would be easy to comply with two names, as had been requested. However, since we had indicated that help was on the way to rid that city of undesirables, he said that he would like to add more names to the list. The two names that the D.A. gave to Hope and I were Ray Lawton and Larry Perkins. He stated that he could name at least two dozen more that should be in prison but they could not be convicted for various reasons. He said that if the project we were working on turned out to be successful, he would welcome the opportunity to supply more names.

We then planned to go next to Windsor and then to Darien. At Windsor Locks we found that the D.A. was very willing to help in any way that he could, and also wanted to submit more than just one name. The name he gave to us was Doug Felder. The D.A. stated that it was known that Felder was involved mainly in the drug trade but was also connected to some of the other illegal activity not only in the city of Windsor Locks but also fairly widespread activity in the state. The D.A. said that he would really be glad to see that person put out of commission.

From there, we proceeded on to Darien where we met with the D.A. These results were about the same as had been in both the cities where we had been in contact with the D.A. Now this D.A. gave the name of Tony Bullock. When we had discussed the problem with the three D.A.s, we had requested that the D.A.s provide us with photos of the individuals and addresses of locations of their residences and any of their frequently visited sites. Each of the D.A.s agreed that this information would be helpful and readily complied. The contacts in these three cities had not consumed much time. So with mission completed, we made plans to go back to the office in Irving. We had discussed this with Admiral Baker and he felt that some of the group should be in the Irving office until the list of twenty-four names could be completed. We would be relieved later and could make a trip to Arizona to get the list of the four undesirables.

Agents Norris and Jones had good results. The two names they got in Manhattan were Edward Sorber and Brian Wright. They then went to Niagara Falls and got the name of Troy Horsely, and then to Albany for the name of Eugene Janick. They also got photos and addresses that were needed. They went on to New Jersey and the cities that they had selected: Newark, New Brunswick, and Atlantic City. The D.A. in each of these cities was very helpful. Norris and Jones felt the D.A.s were very anxious to see if anything could develop as a result of giving them the names, photos, and addresses of places where these people could be found. The names that they gave were Jeff Abel and Cary Moseley in Newark. They've got the name of Morris Gento in New Brunswick and William Newby in Atlantic City. After obtaining the needed information, Norris and Jones headed back to the office in Irving.

Now Agents Small and Watson were on the way to get the names of the four in California. The three cities they chose were Los Angeles, San Francisco, and San Die-go. All of the D.A.s were very anxious to cooperate with Small and Watson. They each had plenty of names they could furnish. The names they got were Ray Andrews and Ed Leon from Los Angeles, Harvey Steele from San Francisco, and Phillip Hatch from San Diego. It took less time to get the needed information from the three D.A.s than they had been expecting.

This assignment completed, they were ready to go to Nevada and secure the names needed from that state. Small and Watson were surprised at the speed at which they were able to complete their goal in these three cities. The names that were supplied to them were Roger Jacobs and Lewis Dwell from Las Vegas, Al Carter from Reno, and Newt Aikens from Carson City. They completed their assignment in Nevada and contacted Hope and me at the office in Irving, where we had been after getting the needed names from Connecticut. Watson said the progress had been so good that she and Small could go ahead and get the needed names from the three cities in Arizona which was okay with Hope and me. We were glad to be relieved to not have to make a trip west.

Agents Small and Watson proceeded to Phoenix. There was no delay in getting two names from the D.A. They were Paul Shannon and Larry Wilton. They then went to Tucson. This was very different. The D.A. there had died a couple of weeks ago and the Assistant D.A. was doing a lot of politicking. It appeared that he really wanted to step up to the D.A. office after the death of the current D.A. He was trying to make a big deal out of the fact that Small and Watson wanted information from him. Watson mentioned to Small that the Assistant D.A. was wanting too much information about the reasoning behind the retrieval of names, so they both agreed that they would skip Tucson and go on to Yuma.

They met with the D.A. in Yuma, told him what information they needed, and they had everything in just a short time. The name they got there was Rusty Johnson. The D.A. said that Johnson was the worst one in the area, but said that he had another—Arnie Green—that he sure did want added to the group of bad people on the list. Watson told the D.A. that she would try to get the name added. That left one more name and one more city to complete the project of names of twenty four undesirables that the group had been asked to get for Admiral Baker.

The two of them headed for Flagstaff. This was the easiest of all. They talked with the D.A. less than thirty minutes. They were given the name of Lance Hansen and were out of Flagstaff and headed on their way back to Irving, Texas.

Agents Norris, Jones, Hope and I were at the office when Small and Watson arrived. After some discussion and guessing as to what Admiral Baker was going to do with the list, all felt that Baker should be contacted and informed that the list was complete.

Admiral Baker was glad that the list was complete. He informed the group in the Irving office that this list should be classified as "Top Secret" and not sent to him in the usual way, but to select two from their group to bring the list to him in Washington and deliver it to him personally. Norris and Jones were selected to deliver the list.

After Baker received the list, he set up a meeting with the two supervisors from the Special Forces group that he had the meeting with a few days ago. He asked Norris and Jones to join him in the meeting.

The main decision derived from the meeting is that the agents would now begin trying to get in place where they would be able to put liquid drops of the poison in something being consumed by each of the twenty-four on the list. They would have a little over four months to get into position to do this, where they can obtain the poison. Then the date for doing this will still be June the first and second.

After this meeting concluded, Baker went back to his office and prepared a message to send to Chester Upchurch. The letter would request the meeting with Baker and the Secretary of Defense, and would be delivered to him by one of the government's special couriers and considered a very secret operation. The courier would be instructed to wait for a reply from Upchurch, and to allow forty-eight hours for a reply. This timetable was included in the message to Upchurch.

The message was prepared and given to the courier. Two days later the courier was in Noumea and ready to deliver the message to Upchurch at his office in Noumea. Upchurch received the courier and said that he would give his answer at the same time the next day.

One would assume that he was trying to determine why a large nation could want to have representatives to meet with him. He did meet with the courier the next day and agreed to meet with the two who were named in the letter. He selected the date of the meeting to be January the twenty-first at 10:00 a.m..

It had been almost a week since the courier had left Washington with the message for Upchurch when he returned with his answer. Admiral Baker was glad that Upchurch agreed to meet with him. He called the Secretary of Defense and told him that the meeting was set for January the twenty-first and Baker asked that he set up their schedule for going on the carrier and destroyer escort so they could comply with the regulations of Bonita.

All of this was done while Norris and Jones were still in Washington. They received all the information and headed back to Irving carrying the message from Baker to the group at the Irving office. The message said, "There was a possibility more murders would be committed, while trying to find solution. We would have to come together on June the first or second and hope to close the case."

Meanwhile, the entire Irving group was needed at the border crossing from Mexico to the U.S.A. They would continue to help until May the fifteenth. The message went on to say why the group was needed: it seems the House of Representatives and the Senate wanted to pass a bill that would help illegal aliens enter our country. The President vetoed this bill and they overrode his veto. The bill said that illegals from Mexico would be identified and returned to their country. All other aliens would be identified and given green cards and released but requested to report to an immigration officer after they had found a job and had an address. This caused the illegals, other than the ones from Mexico, to waive their hands at the officials so that they could be taken into custody, given a green card and then released.

Our Baker's Dozen team all agreed that this was a problem only the Politicians in Washington could solve.

FOURTEEN

Ray Coffee, a resident of both California and Texas, who had become extremely wealthy from dealing in oil stocks, land, and other investments. Coffee had decided to use some of that wealth to correct the injustice this bill's burden that southern states. Coffee had set up a meeting with his accountants and lawyers to retrieve their opinion on the plan that he had devised. It was this: he would form a non-profit corporation, "Aid to Aliens" (A.T.A), with the goal to help expedite the new law concerning illegal aliens. They would assist these people to locate in the U.S. and give them a small amount of money while being assisted by the city government of the new location securing employment. The real reason was to get these illegals out of the southern states. After the non-profit corporation was chartered, he obtained a ruling from the I.R.S. that contributions to the corporation would be tax-deductible. After all of this was set up, Coffee met with about twenty of his closest friends and explained the real reason for ATA which was to help the aliens relocate to the city of their choice. He said that we would help them in the selection of the city. Perhaps they would like to locate in the same city of the sponsor and co-sponsor of the alien bill. They wanted to thank their people for help in locating the jobs that they had promised when they were trying to persuade other representatives to vote for the bill. The aliens would have to make a signed statement of these facts. This cooperation would also have a humanitarian goal, and that would be to assist Mexicans that had been detained after crossing the border illegally. Help would be given them to return to Mexico. When the twenty heard these reasons for the non-profit tax-deductible corporation, they made some sizeable donations and then made plans to call several of their contacts, both business and social. In just less than thirty days, this new corporation was one of the wealthiest charitable establishments in the United States.

Coffee put his plan in motion. They first contacted immigration at three locations and told them that their new company could take 120 illegals per day, and they would make three flights a week, one each to Cancun, Mazatlan, and Acapulco.

Of course the real reason for selecting three locations was to make it more difficult for them to make the trip back to the border, and also to let the Mexican government know what a problem this is to the U.S.

The company would work with immigration, and after the illegals had been given a green card, they would be offered a plane ride and a small amount of money to help them in relocation while they were waiting for aid in the new city. The first 120 to leave the border would go to Albany, New York, the home of Senator Hap Gentry, one of the co-sponsors of the bill. Each of the aliens would be given the address and the phone number of Hap Gentry, who had said, when trying to get this bill passed, that city in the U.S. should be glad to accept these aliens into their community because there is a shortage of unskilled labor.

The second 120 went to Pittsburg, Pennsylvania, the home of the other co-sponsor, Senator Edward Moseley. There were enough illegals coming across the border to make two trips a week to both Albany and Pittsburg. All of this new action, issuing green cards and releasing aliens, had made it more difficult for Mexicans to enter into the U.S. at unguarded locations.

So the illegal immigrants had been trying to find ways to cross the border checkpoints. This is why the six agents from Irving had gone back to help the Border Patrol find other ways to stop them from entering the U.S.

Senator Hap Gentry and Edward Moseley sure had a change of mind after the second plane-load of aliens had entered their city. Both had received phone calls from the new aliens in their city. Some had even tried to contact them at their homes. After the second week of this plan Coffee had put into motion, both of these senators were in Washington trying to determine how they could stop this action.

The actions taken by the A.T.A. were completely legal. They could not do anything legally to stop the activity.

They would have to admit to their fellow senators that they were wrong in passing the bill, and to make the last bill void, or a new one to make changes. A bill was introduced that would make it illegal to admit anyone the way that the previous bill had suggested. The new bill was passed in record time.

Coffee stopped assisting illegals to go to the cities of their choice, but continued to send the Mexicans to the three locations in Mexico. Coffee and his group continued with the so-called assistance to illegals. The officials at each of these cities that were receiving the illegals back to their country were complaining to their government about the procedure being implemented by the Ray Coffee group. These three cities were getting a lot of unskilled labor and also many people who had recently been released from prison. They were actually witnessing what had been happening at the various points of entry in border cities along the Mexican border across the United States. This procedure continued by the Ray Coffee group. The Mexican government did nothing to stop these illegals from being returned or to stop the illegals from entering the United States. Even with the return of these illegals, the Mexican government was still getting rid of a great number of undesirables and unskilled people.

FIFTEEN

Six agents from Irving were still working with the Border Patrol. Admiral Baker was waiting to go to Bonita Island, where he and Roger Walker, the U.S. Secretary of Defense, would meet with Chester Upchurch on the twenty-first of January at ten a.m. It was decided that Walker would contact the admiral in charge of the Pacific Fleet and confirm the arrangement that had been set up for the aircraft carrier and the destroyer escort. Baker and Walker would arrive aboard a military transport at Henderson Field, Guadalcanal, on the eighteenth of January, and then be transported by helicopter to the aircraft carrier that would be located in the immediate area. The aircraft carrier and also the destroyer escort would be located off the southwest coast of Guadalcanal, near Cape Hunter. Since World War II, all of the larger vessels had stayed clear of the area known as Iron Bottom Bay. The selected location did not create any problems since it could be made in reasonable time by helicopter. Admiral Baker told Walker that it sure looked as if the plan would allow plenty of time to make the connections at the appointed time. Walker's reply was that he had always enjoyed being on an aircraft carrier, and this would allow some time for pleasure. He said his schedule kept him very busy, so he was taking advantage of this time to slow down and enjoy being on the carrier. Baker agreed that Walker had made a good choice and they would enjoy some time at a slower pace. This plan would not alert the crew that anything special was taking place. Both vessels would proceed to a position about two miles from Bonita Island.

They would arrive at the location in the afternoon of January the twentieth, so there would be no problem being on time for the ten a.m. meeting on the following day. The officers of the two vessels would have to be told of a reason for going to Bonita Island. It was decided they would be told that some very important experiments were being conducted on the island. This was true. However, the experiments were pertaining to diet and a way of life and were not of a military nature. So as far as the officers of the two vessels knew, this was a good-will visit with the owner of the island.

The six agents Hope, Norris, Jones, Small, Watson, and I were working with the Border Patrol to making changes daily in our methods to curtail illegals from crossing our borders.

Meanwhile, Baker was departing for the planned meeting on the island of Bonita, He contacted two supervisors of the Special Forces group. He informed them the time of the meeting that had been set up for himself and Walker to meet with Chester Upchurch. He was informed the twenty-four agents that were all trying to get positioned where they could administer the poison to their selected subjects on the first or second of June. Five of the twenty-four were already in their location where they would be in contact with the selected subjects on that date. The remainder of the twenty-four agents reported that they were making progress and all felt that it would be possible to accomplish the goal on the first or second of June. Baker knew that it was going to be hard to complete this task on a certain date, and that is why he selected two dates. This poison works within twenty-four hours, so it is possible to administer some on the first and then others on the second before any results could be observed. He was pleased with the plan.

Now all that remained was to meet with Upchurch and persuade him to agree to help by allowing someone from Baker's group to obtain enough poison to complete this plan.

Baker and Walker left Washington by helicopter to Camp David in Maryland. There they would board one of the old Air Force One planes. The powers in Washington did not want the general public to know about the poison or its intended use.

The U.S. has three fully-equipped planes that are exactly like Air Force One the President uses when he travels. Three planes have been proven to be a good plan, for instance, if one is down for repairs or maintenance check, there is always one that is ready to be airborne at a very short notice. Since these are constantly being replaced with newer planes at the rate of three at a time, the three older planes are available for government use by some of the higher ranking officials in Washington. This takes three out of the service, and these planes have so much secret equipment installed that it is more advisable to destroy the complete plane than to try to remove everything. Baker and Walker would fly direct to Henderson Field at Guadalcanal and from there by helicopter to the aircraft carrier, and later transferred to the destroyer escort to tie up at the dock at Bonita Island.

Shortly after leaving Camp David, Baker and Walker compared notes about how they would convey their message to Chester Upchurch. They must have gone through at least fifteen ideas before they both agreed on a message to present to Upchurch that would allow the U.S. to get the poison off of his island. After both had agreed on the message for Upchurch, there was not much to occupy their time on this long flight. Both took advantage of the time and read, and both had a few naps. The flight was uneventful and tiring. They were really glad when they touched down at Henderson Field.

The plan was that they would have some discussions with the top brass in the area, and especially the officer in charge of the air operations. They were going to have these meetings so everyone would think that this was just like other meetings where the people from Washington would make nonscheduled visits to their remote locations. It was amazing to both Baker and Walker how the area of the airfield and the surrounding property had developed since either of them had been on Guadalcanal. They took some time to visit various sites on the air field and had lunch with some of those in charge of various operations at the base. Time moved quickly, a helicopter was sent to transport Walker and Baker to the carrier.

They enjoyed visiting with some of their old friends and hearing about the good things that were happening at the remote South Pacific location.

The helicopter arrived for the brief trip to the carrier. Upon arriving on the carrier deck, they were escorted to the meeting room for the ship's officers. There was a separate briefing room for the pilots. Here they were greeted by the captain of the carrier who was an old friend of both Baker and Walker. Two other officers were there. One of these was known to Baker and the other was an old friend of Walker's. Walker led the discussion. He knew every man in the room was curious as to why he and Baker were making a visit to this location. Walker related to them this was just one of the locations they would be visiting on this trip. Walker wanted to see for himself what the conditions were at these particular locations.

The major reason to make this trip was to include a visit to the island of Bonita. "They are conducting some tests on the island that our government is very interested in." Walker said.

Both Baker and Walker felt that it would be assumed by officers in the room, that they were military tests, he left them to draw their own conclusions and did not tell them the tests were really how to live a healthy life by eating proper food, good sleeping habits, and a rigorous exercise program.

Walker felt sure the three accepted the explanations for this visit, and he did plan to make two or three visits to military locations on the way back to the U.S.A. They made a tour of some of the stations on the carrier so it would look quite natural checking these areas.

Later they had the evening meal with the captain and the Executive Officer and a few officers. After the meal and some time for visitation, Baker and Walker retired for the evening. The sea was calm and they had a good night's rest.

After breakfast the next morning, they were in the Control Room along with the captain when they received an S.O.S. from a vessel that was sinking. The location that had been given was close to the carrier. This would have been hard to determine a few years ago, but with the use of global positioning devices that they now have, the exact location was given along with the S.O.S. The captain notified other vessels in the area that a helicopter was being dispatched and would send additional help if needed. Nothing was indicated in the S.O.S. to determine the size of the vessel or how many were on board. It seemed like a very long time before any message was received from the helicopter, but it was actually thirty-five minutes. They reported they had located a life raft with four aboard and would make an attempt to lift each of them aboard the helicopter. They reported that the vessel that sent the S.O.S. had not been located and they assumed that it had sunk. A report would follow if the four in the life raft had been airlifted to the helicopter. The next contact with the crew on the helicopter reported that all four had been rescued from the lifeboat and seemed to be in good shape and did not need emergency care. They were now on their way back to the aircraft carrier.

This was an unusual sight for Walker, but Baker had witnessed many rescues similar to this. However, most rescues at sea were caused by very bad weather. They were all anxious to learn what had caused that vessel to sink.

Although the rescued crew from the sunken vessel seemed to be in a non-life-threatening condition, they were checked over by the carrier medical team before they were asked to report the cause of the sinking of the vessel. Both Baker and Walker were present, along with the captain of the carrier, when the four told of the event that caused the sinking of their vessel. The four consisted of two couples that appeared to be in their early sixties. They said that they were having breakfast, the sea was calm, and they had not seen anything unusual in their vicinity. The vessel was a fairly good-sized sailboat with sleeping quarters. They felt a great bump and almost immediately started taking on water. The bump was caused by a very large floating log that had rammed them. The log looked more like a very big utility pole. It is very unusual to see an object like they had described floating in the open water. Even if the four of them had been very observant, the log would have been very hard to detect.

Most of the time anything that ends up in the sea after a storm will wash up on the shore on some island very soon after the storm has passed.

They immediately sent out an S.O.S. with a G.P.S. location and could do nothing to save the vessel. After they had completed their report, they revealed some personal information. Both of the couples had lived and worked in the San Diego area. One of the men had been in the Marines during World War II and had been sent to Noumea for a two week rest before returning to duty. He especially liked the area, so when he retired, both he and his wife were so excited about the possibility of moving to Noumea for their golden years. Their longtime friends decided to join them in the adventure. It took some time to be able to make the move. After they were in Noumea for a few months, they made a plan. One couple purchased a home that could provide some privacy for each couple. The other couple purchased a sailboat that would accommodate all four and possibly two or three guests. They selected this plan so there would not be any problem if they had a disagreement. In that event, each couple had their own property and there wouldn't be any problem with division of assets.

The captain informed the four that the carrier would be within thirty-five miles of Noumea the next morning and a helicopter would transport them to Noumea. The captain said he would furnish them with a copy of the activity during the rescue, in the event it was needed for the report for insurance purposes.

The next morning the ship was located a few miles off the Coast of Bonita Island and Baker and Walker were prepared to meet with Upchurch. One helicopter left the carrier with the four people that had been rescued and preceded to Noumea. Baker and Walker boarded another helicopter and were transported to the destroyer escort so they could tie up at the dock at Bonita Island. Baker and Walker had both viewed satellite photos of the island. Everything seemed to be first class. But they were shocked at what they saw first as the destroyer escort was securing the mooring line.

The dock and everything that was in view from the ship was that of a very expensive resort property. The dock had not been built by local laborers. It was A-1 construction, something what you would find at any of the U.S. Naval bases.

After going ashore, they were met by Albert James, who explained, "He was the assistant to Mr. Upchurch, and he would take them directly to a meeting room where he would join them." So far, everything appeared as what had been explained to them about the surroundings they found themselves in.

All the people on the island they had seen were slim and trim, something like you would see in an old Fred Astaire and Ginger Rogers movie. It was hard to believe, but everyone that they saw appeared to be in very good health. That is, if being slim and trim was any indication.

While they were waiting for Upchurch, they were offered coffee, but no donuts! This was not the custom in the U.S.

They didn't have to wait long. Upchurch came in and was introduced by James. He looked slim and trim just like the rest of the islanders. Baker and Walker had decided that since Walker was Secretary of Defense, it would be good if he led discussion with Upchurch.

Walker started off with the usual praise of how good it was of Upchurch to meet with us but then stated the reason for the meeting.

He said, "It was well known that the rules of the island were very fair but also extremely strict." He continued, "But one of your previous guests has found a way to take some of the juice from the rainbow ball fruit off of the island. We know the name of the guest."

Walker proceeded to asked, "We are prepared to reveal the name of this person if you would be willing to help us solve and find a solution to a serious problem in the states."

Mr. Upchurch took a sip of coffee and said, "Please continue, you have my complete attention."

Walker sat in a chair directly facing Mr. Upchurch, and continued, "We have a number of undesirables in the United States. These people are involved in the selling of drugs, dealing in stolen merchandise, and murder. We have tried but cannot get enough information on them to get a conviction in a trial. Even though we know that they would be given the death sentence if brought to the trial.

We know you have a poison on this island that produces death in twenty-four hours. The reason that we know this is that we have investigated several deaths that have had large insurance policies and these deaths have been classified as cause unknown. We have been observing several of the people who are suspected of being involved in these cases. We have come to the conclusion it could only be one person who is a frequent visitor and somehow has found a way to get the poison off of your island."

Walker glanced at Baker for approval before continuing, "Mr. Upchurch, the person who has been identified as removing poison from your island is Justin Price. What we would like to do is eliminate those people in the U.S. who are using the poison for their gain. We would like to have your permission to remove enough poison to eliminate these people. Our plan is to remove enough poison to take out several criminals who are definitely guilty of the worst crimes, but we are unable to convict. In exchange for your help, even though you are independent of any country, we would consider you as a favored nation. If you agree with this, we would like to work out a plan where we would get twenty-four vials of the poison on May the fifteenth. This would give us time to get the poison to the agents who are in position to administer the poison to twenty-four selected evil people. This project will only be known by a few selected people. If this is successful, we would like to repeat the plan again in six months."

Upchurch immediately agreed to the plan. He also stated that if Price made plans to come back to his island before the May fifteenth time of pickup, that he would not want us to prevent him from making a trip to his island for the one-week stay. He said that he remembered Price because he has been on the island several times. Others have been several times for the week stay. They all say they kept coming back because they had such a good time. He went on to say that if Price is the one who has been taking poison off the island, this would be confirmed on this next visit.

They continued discussion and worked out the type of containers for the poison. Baker informed Upchurch that the twenty-four containers would be furnished and would be shipped to his office in Noumea. The outside container will have the appearance of a briefcase.

They then took a very short tour of the island and came back and had lunch. Be-fore Baker and Walker left, Upchurch requested that the two of them return on May the fifteenth to make the pickup of the poison. He said that he would welcome them to stay a couple of days and enjoy the hospitality and see how their daily activities affect their health, looks and over all wellbeing.

As Baker and Walker were leaving Bonita Island and going to the destroyer escort, they expressed to each other that the meeting was much better than either of them had anticipated. Both agreed to make plans to have extra time for a two-day visit when they returned on May the fifteenth. They were soon transferred by helicopter from the destroyer escort to the aircraft carrier for their trip back to Guadalcanal, and then back to the States.

The trip back to Washington was long, boring, and extremely uneventful. Baker and Walker were glad to be home. This trip had caused both of them to fall behind on their scheduled meetings and responsibilities. It didn't take but a few days to get back to normal.

Baker contacted one of the two supervisors for the Special Forces group, Robert O'Grady. The other supervisor was Walt Carter and was not available to meet with Baker and O'Grady. They met in an office that had been checked for listening devises to make sure what was said in the room, stayed in the room!

Baker informed O'Grady about the meeting with Upchurch at Bonita Island, and that Upchurch had agreed

to furnish the needed poison. Baker explained the need
for twenty-four containers and a case that would prevent
damage to the containers on a trip to the U.S.A. Also, Baker
thought it would be a good idea to make twenty-four extra
containers to distribute to the agents to make sure that these
would be suitable to aid in the completion of their mission.
O'Grady agreed that the agents should have advanced
knowledge about the containers that were going to carry the
poison. He said that he would have their lab work on this
project and he would meet with Carter to brief him about
the plan. He agreed to contact Baker as soon as the lab had
a plan for getting the poison back to the U.S. Upchurch had
agreed that it would be a good idea to furnish one ounce
of poison for each of the twenty-four containers that were
needed. This would be enough back-up in the event that the
first or second attempt to administer the poison was not a
success.

Baker contacted me and informed me that the
insurance project was developing as planned. I relayed
the information that great progress was being made at the
border crossings. We were seeing fewer illegals trying to
cross at the checkpoints. We were now working to locate
and stop the drug trade from getting any of those shipments
past the checkpoints.

The Border Patrol had increased their aerial patrols, and
by notifying ground patrols they had located and stopped
many illegal people and drugs from entering our country.
Baker wanted all six of us to be in the Irving office on May
the fifteenth.

Baker talked with me, and said," he was considering
what direction to take the case." He wanted to get a report
on the progress of the twenty-four agents that were trying
to be in position to administer the poison on June the first
or second.

He planned that Al Gotto would not be included in the plan for elimination. Baker is very aware how the mafia thinks.

He said, "When any of the mafia members are murdered, they always suspect the rival gangs for the killings."

Gotto and his group knew all about the insurance plans they have in place and the names of the individuals that have been selected to be killed.

Although Gotto will probably not be eliminated in this action, he will be very nervous about his well-being, when those who work for him, begin to die. Upchurch is in agreement with Baker's plan to repeat this process at a later date. They can take care of Gotto at some time in the future. In the meantime, Gotto will be so nervous he will have a lot of undesirables eliminated and save us a lot of time and expense.

Baker asked for a progress report from O'Grady and Carter, the two supervisors from Special Forces that are in charge of the twenty-four agents that plan to administer the poison on June the first or second. Baker got a message from O'Grady that the package was ready. This meant that the twenty-four containers and the cases containing the poison were ready.

O'Grady said, "How do you plan the agents to be in position on time to disperse the poison in June?"

Carter informed O'Grady they would have all the necessary information, and when everything had been planned and approved they set up a meeting for Thursday at 10:00am at the same room that is continually used as a safe and secure place and made their final plans to distribute the poison.

Meanwhile, back at the border Baker's agents are at the three border crossings from Mexico into the U.S.A. were making progress in slowing down the amount of illegal people and drugs passing through the checkpoints were now being detected. The people who are trying to get the drugs across the border and into the U.S.A. keep coming up with new ways to try to fool the inspector at the border. It didn't take long for the inspectors to become aware of the new methods being used to get drugs past the check point.

As soon as the drugs and shipments are located, the drug cartel develops a new method to try and smuggle their illegal drugs through the border crossing. The case unfolded like this: the drugs took some time to detect. Fertilizer from a company that has several huge chicken farms in Mexico ship a lot of fertilizer to the U.S. This is in heavy plastic bags, only forty pounds each. But even though the product is sealed in bags, a truck-load has a very unpleasant odor. A company from Mexico has been placing plastic-wrapped containers of drugs in containers with the fertilizer. They probably assume that because of the odor, none of the inspectors would be interested in making a thorough inspection of the shipment.

They were right. They got away with this method for some time. What got the attention of the inspector was increasing frequency of these shipments. When the inspectors finally got up enough nerve to brave the odor and make a thorough inspection, they were amazed at the volume of drugs being sent to the U.S. by this method. Needless to say, the drug cartel immediately came up with new ways to get through the border crossing without being detected. The most effective method for drug control through the border crossing was the G.P.S. device on the vehicle that could be picked up after they thought they had fooled the authorities. We had a lot of electronic equipment to help locate these drug shipments. The Border Patrol had good detection devices and dogs locate drugs in difficult places.

They were making arrests daily and the vehicles that were transporting the drugs were being impounded and later sold. This was a minor inconvenience for these people. Losing vehicles was no problem because they were making so much money and they would just buy more equipment. The people being arrested meant nothing to those in charge of shipping the drugs. There were many people waiting for a chance to get involved in this process.

Back in Washington, Baker met with O'Grady and Carter on Thursday at ten a.m. O'Grady had the twenty four vials in the carrying case that had been designed to carry the poison from Bonita Island to the U.S. He also had one of the vials, or containers, which would be given to each of the twenty-four agents so they would know how the poison would be furnished to them. Baker approved of all of this. He took control of the container and the twenty-four bottles that the poison was to be shipped in from the island. He notified the government courier to deliver this as a package-unit to the office that Upchurch maintained in Noumea.

Before they left the safe room, O'Grady informed Baker of the progress being made of the twenty-four, and how they planned to administer the poison to the selected subjects. Three of the twenty-four had been able to become cooks at small restaurants where subjects would have coffee and donuts every morning. These were very small restaurants with several stools along the counter. The cooks and waitresses both served the customers at the counter. Strange, but all three of the subjects liked to have end seats at each of the restaurants. Two of the agents had gone to work for their subjects and were with them during the noon meal every day.

All five of these reported that it should be possible to administer poison to the selected subjects on the appointed date. The remaining nineteen of the twenty-four agents reported that they were making progress in being in position to administer the poison on June the first or second. But no date was firm just yet. O'Grady and Carter told Baker, "All the agents should be able to complete their mission on either one of the two dates that had been agreed upon."

Baker left the meeting with a good feeling about the success of the plan they had put into motion.

SIXTEEN

The six agents at the border crossing were making progress in locating both illegal individuals and drugs at the checkpoint. So much of the traffic had to be diverted to areas that were not so heavily guarded. This created more activity for Coffee and his group they were intercepting the illegals and sending them back to Mexico. His group was finding that more of the illegals were trying to bring more drugs into the U.S. through these routes. He and the team have been successfully curtailing these illegal activities.

Baker received a new report about several more deaths. All the victims had a large insurance policy and the cause of death was unknown. He knew his group was working as hard as they possibly could to stop this criminal activity. We had to have concrete evidence in order to arrest the perpetrators.

Baker felt sure their plan would be successful on the first and second of June. He said, "Al Gotto had not been included in the group that would have the poison administered to them in June. He was still of the opinion that when some of their group were eliminated, the assumption by the gang would be that rival gangs had done them in, and they would start killing each other. This would make his job easier, and also give him satisfaction that his plan had been a success."

Walker contacted Admiral Baker about the trip back to Bonita Island on May the fifteenth. Walker said it had been some time since anyone from Washington had visited the U.S. Samoa Islands, or "American Samoa" and that he thought it would be a good idea to take extra time on this trip and include a stopover at Samoa. Baker agreed and said he would enjoy the time visiting with the governor of American Samoa, since he was a very good, long-time friend of his, and also had known Walker for several years.

They made plans to include this side trip and he scheduled it prior to meeting with Upchurch on the fifteenth of May.

Baker contacted the six agents that were helping the Border Patrol to try to control the amount of drugs and illegal people at the border crossings. He encouraged the six to continue to do everything they could to help the border agents and to stay until May the fifteenth, when they would return to the office in Irving.

Activity in Washington was mainly the usual routine for Baker in the days prior to departure for the visit to the location in the Pacific. He had a meeting with O'Grady and Carter. He was briefed about the progress of the twenty-four agents that were trying to be in position to administer the poison to the selected subjects on June the first or second. The last report said that nineteen of the twenty-four were making progress, but nothing firm. There were still just three in good position. Now they were reporting that out of these nineteen, there are four that just have not been able to get into position to accomplish the goal. The four agents are trying to get close to, Ed Leon in Los Angeles, Phillip Hatch in San Diego, Newt Aikens in Carson City, and Paul Shannon in Phoenix. Baker told O'Grady and Carter to get a plan to take care of these four in the event our agents are unable to be in position in time for action on the first of June.

It was soon time for Baker and Walker to depart to Washington for the visit to the location in the Pacific. They touched down in American Samoa at eleven in the morning. Samoa time. This was the first visit to Samoa for

Walker. Baker had been to the islands several times. But this would be the first time since Theodore Hastings had been governor of the American Samoa.

Hastings had sent his car and driver to meet and escort them to the Governor's Palace. This was a beautiful, well-constructed white building that overlooked a dock and beach area. Baker remembered that there had been a lot of crime and drugs and a lot of other illegal activity at the time Theodore Hastings became governor of American Samoa. Baker knew conditions had been bad enough that most of the travel agencies recommend that tourists avoid that location. And also, many cruise ships stopped coming to the area because it was unsafe.

This was reason enough for a change in command and Hastings had been selected to be the new governor. He was anxious to find out about the current conditions.

On the short trip from the airport to the Governor's Mansion, Baker observed that conditions must be a lot better, since he noticed quite a few tourists, both at the airport and in view from their car as they made their way to the house that the governor called home. Hastings was really glad to see both Baker and Walker. The visit was listed as a meeting with, Baker and Walker, Good-Will Ambassadors from the President of the United States. Hastings knew that, but he also knew that both of these men would consider this to be more of a personal visit. This could be recorded as an official visit from representatives of the President of the U.S.

As they entered the governor's home, Walker was amazed at the beauty of this structure. This was a great day and they immediately went outside to tables and chairs on the lawn so that they could enjoy the weather and the great view. They were served refreshments and Baker made the comment that indications are the conditions are better than when Hastings took over as governor. Hastings said that crime rates were down, there were very little drugs, and other illegal activities had been curtailed.

The next question proposed by Baker was, "How did you accomplish this, and could your methods be adapted to some of our cities in the U.S?"

Hastings said he had to make a lot of changes, "There is a prison here capable of holding fifteen hundred prisoners. When I first came to the island, there were only three people locked up. The three were what you would call 'political prisoners,' so I had them released. The building of the prison was well constructed. It had very thick walls that aided in insulation. It needed some cleaning and new paint, and the kitchen needed to be updated. I had these changes made so that we could accommodate a total of fifteen hundred prisoners if needed. Next, I temporarily abolished the authority of the smaller courts and notified by radio, ads and circulars, that certain crime would be handled by a governor's court. These crimes included dealing drugs; possession of illegal substances; any crime against a tourist; being a foreigner without a passport; rape; and murder. Also included, would be any police officer who fails to do his duty when he observes any illegal activities."

Needless to say, shortly after this went into effect we had some test cases. The first one was a known drug dealer. The dealer was caught peddling marijuana. He was arrested and placed in jail. Under my ruling, he is not permitted to talk with any outsider. He was brought to my court the next day. He felt that he deserved just a slap on the wrist; what he received was a yearlong visit to our newly remodeled and updated prison. He would have no visitors and would be assigned to the work detail. His cohorts tried to get lawyers from Australia, New Zealand and New Caledonia, but they all found out it was useless to come here because our court makes the decision is final.

"Some people have a hard time with facts. We soon had over four hundred in that prison that are mostly drug dealers and thieves. My staff and I had several meetings with the few judges that would normally handle these types of cases. We were mainly concerned with how to handle these criminals after they were released from prison. One of the judges came up with an idea that we all agreed would be effective. He said that of the several smaller islands that are in this area, and owned by the U.S., there is one called 'Rocky Island' that is not very desirable. This island is populated but everything is very primitive. The judge suggested that when a prisoner is released after their one year sentence he should be notified that if he should be involved in criminal activity the result would be isolated on Rocky Island. Of course we knew the history of Rocky Island, but he repeated this information for us. Basically, there's a strange current between our location and Rocky Island. The current tends to push everything back towards Rocky Island. It is impossible to leave the island by boat that is powered only by human effort.

"There is one other known island that has this type of current. It is one of the is-lands in the Hawaiian group. It has many vessels on its beaches and in the waters nearby that have been caught in the current. That area in Hawaii is referred to as the 'Pacific Graveyard.'

"We accepted his plan and it has helped us with the crime problem. The citizens and tourists feel safer. We currently have less than fifty people in our prison. Well that's enough about that. I want to know about your recent activities."

Walker told him this trip was a little unusual for him as Secretary of Defense to be making. Walker went on to explain Guadalcanal would be visited and that he was going to be with Baker when they made an unusual visit to an island close to New Caledonia.

Baker took over the conversation and said, "Both of them were to visit with the owner of Bonita, the small island Walker mentioned. Bonita is not a possession of any country. It is privately owned, and we are treating the owner just as we would the leader of any nation. There are some very important medical tests being conducted on that island and the U.S. is very interested in the results."

Baker and Walker both failed to mention the true reason for the visit with Up-church. Everything was peaceful and seemed to be at a slow pace. This was obvious when it seemed the time they were having lunch, one thirty, was a usual time. Their lunch was served on a terrace. Baker was thinking that even though there were a lot of problems being the American governor of American Samoa, Hastings had a pretty good life.

After lunch, Hastings took them on a short tour of the island and they returned late in the afternoon. They had time to relax, having a refreshing shower, and later they joined Hastings and some of the staff for drinks on the terrace. The weather was great and the view was unbelievable. The group that Hastings had assembled for the evening social and meal were some of the most influential people of the island, including two from just west of the hundred seventy-first meridian of west longitude.

This territory is officially known as the "Territory of Western Samoa." Over the years it has been governed by Germany, New Zealand, Britain, and even as a United Nations trust territory. The port of Pago Pago on the island of Tutuila is the location of the governor's operation center. On the most important island of American Samoa, the meal in the evening was very enjoyable. Baker and Walker agreed that it was good they had made this good-will stop while on their way to meet with Upchurch on the island of Bonita. After the activity of the evening they had a good night's rest, and after breakfast the next morning they boarded a military plane for the next phase of their journey, with the destination of Henderson Field, Guadalcanal.

Shortly after touching down at Henderson Field they boarded a helicopter for the trip to the aircraft carrier that was close by and ready to transport Baker and Walker to

Bonita Island. For their meeting with Chester Upchurch, Walker had mentioned to Baker about some of the difficulties that he, as Secretary of Defense, had encountered in dealing with some of the leaders of countries around the world. The nice thing about dealing with Upchurch was he could make a decision without having to get an okay from anyone. They were both looking forward to the time they were going to be guests of Upchurch on his island. The last time that they had visited the island of Bonita aboard the carrier, there had been a rescue made of a vessel in distress. Nothing exciting happened on this trip, and the timing was perfect to be prepared to go ashore at the appointed time. They contacted Bonita Island by radio and did the proper thing and asked for permission to tie up at the dock. Permission was granted and they boarded the destroyer escort, leaving the carrier in full view of the dock area of Bonita.

Upon stepping onto shore, they were again greeted by Albert James who said, "I will take you directly to your cabin, and after you have a chance to freshen up and relax you can join Upchurch and I in the central meeting room."

When Baker and Walker returned to the central meeting room, Upchurch was present with James and told them he had complied with their request and had received the package containing the vials to transport the poison. He said he felt certain our agent who had visited his island had relayed all information about poison, but he would repeat it to be certain that information had been correct. He did not use as much detail as Mr. James related to the weekly guests. He just gave the highlights. He explained that the fruit that is called "Rainbow Ball" is first green as it develops. As it ripens, it becomes white. And when ripe and edible it is orange. This can only be eaten when it is orange and no white is showing on the skin.

Upchurch said, "When ripe, it is probably the best fruit that is available from any country. However, eating it anytime other than orange, it will kill you. There will not be any indication that you have eaten anything that disagrees with you. You will not get sick. You will just die within twenty four hours." Upchurch changed the subject by informing them, "The evening meal will be served at a different, scenic location that I'm sure you will remember for a long time."

Upchurch and James wanted to escort Baker and Walker on a short tour before making their way to the location for dinner. They all boarded a vehicle for a fifteen minute trip to a fenced-in area that Upchurch explained this is where some of the experiments are being conducted by one of the universities in the U.S. He explained the fence was to make certain that no one disturbed the procedure being conducted there. They made a right turn and continued along the fence until they reached another gate that was controlled by an electric gate opener. Mr. James explained that deliveries were made at this location. Also, there is a location next to the social or meeting area where the subjects can be observed by way of a one-way mirror, similar to what they have in some prisons in the U.S.

"We and the medical team can observe at any time without being detected. We will see some of the ten people that are subjects of the study. These people all have various types of non-contagious diseases. Each one has been classified as terminal—with less than six months to live. All continue to have medication that that was pre-scribed for them in the U.S. This group has been here about nine months now. They are living just like the citizens of our island are living except they have contact with no one outside of the test area. They are kept active. All are past the predicted time of death. This study was to determine what, if anything, has helped them. Was it the absence of radio, television, additive in food, too much rest, or any other thing that could be determined? As you will observe, some of these are a little overweight, but most, after nine months here look about like our islanders. All report that they are feeling better than they have in years." Upchurch said that he wanted Baker and Walker to see this and to think about ways to help the American citizens to become healthier. They observed for a while and then left and stopped at the rest area located next to the cog train.

Baker and Walker did just like all of the other guests had done when they saw the cog train. They looked amazed to see something like this on a remote island in the Pacific and after being told that they would board the train for a short trip, they were anxious to see what was at the other end of the rail line that the cog train traveled. Baker observed that everything on the island was first-class construction. It was just as Agent Jones had reported after her visit to the island a few months before this. Baker and Walker had observed that there were only two guests on the island during this time.

Walker asked Upchurch about the two, and Upchurch replied that no other guests had been scheduled for this week. He said that due to the purpose of Baker and Walker's visit, he felt that it would be best to keep it private so that the U.S. State Department wouldn't have to answer to many questions about the visit to his island.

They soon reached the top of the hill. The scene was outstanding. In the distance you could see three small islands and an unbelievable sunset. The building next to the train stop was very modern and well-constructed, just like everything they had previously seen.

It all looks like it would last a hundred years, and maybe more. After taking in the view for a while, they entered the building. This was a very large building with about half designed as a meeting room and the other half, as a dining room. Baker observed that the dining room was fully staffed and this seemed odd, since the four that came up on the cog train would be the only ones to eat a meal this evening. Mr. James said normally this dining room was just open one evening per week. The exception was when Upchurch had guest visiting him here on the island.

Mr. James began to talk about the meal that would be served to them this evening. "Almost everything was grown here on the island. There are some exceptions: flour, sugar, seasonings, spices, and so forth. Most of the food and all of the meat is a product of this island. After many months of pressure, Mr. Upchurch agreed to export some of the canned products. The meat is fast-frozen and shipped to select upscale restaurants in the U.S. You will be eating meat that any health food market in the U.S. would be delighted to have available to sell to their customers. None of the food that we produce here has had any type of chemicals added to soil or sprayed on the produce. The animals have been given pure grains and none have been given hormones of any type or shots. When you taste this food you will realize that this is one of the reasons none of the islanders have any desire to leave this island."

They left the lounge area and went on to the dining room. Soon they were eating and Baker and Walker expressed to Upchurch that this was absolutely the best meal that they had ever eaten in their entire life. Both said that they had been to some dinners at the White House where they had very famous chefs, but nothing compared to this. Upchurch explained since they would be leaving mid-afternoon tomorrow, he wanted to make a short visit to the ranch so they could see just how healthy the animals were when they were raised without all the chemicals that are used in the U.S. He also stated that lunch would be served at the ranch.

They stayed and visited for a while after the meal and then took the cog train back down the hill and then returned to their assigned cabins, turned in, and had a good night's rest.

The next morning Upchurch and James were there to greet them at the dining area. They ate breakfast together and discussed plans for the day. After enjoying the view and another cup of coffee, the four of them left for a trip to the ranch. It was several miles to the ranch. Baker was amazed at the conditions of the roads. A person would think that this was a very expensive resort that catered only to the very rich. The road was a clean and well-constructed concrete strip that was plenty wide for two vehicles to travel on.

They soon reached the main ranch road. This, too, was constructed of better material than had been expected. They met Guy Duke who escorted Baker and Walker on a tour of the headquarters area. It was obvious that Up-church had planned everything that was constructed on the island going to last for a very long time. After this tour was complete, they returned to the main ranch house, where they would have their noon meal. The five of them talked for a while about the things that were being done to have healthy animals on the ranch.

Baker had several questions about how they prevented certain animal diseases. Upchurch had questions about how things were being done in the U.S. After much information had been exchanged, they were served a meal that in the States would be called a working man's meal. Everything was good, and Baker and Walker thought even though some of the food would be the same as served in the U.S., the taste was superior!

After lunch, Baker, Walker, and Duke took a final tour of the ranch land. The vehicle looked as if it could withstand an earthquake. It looked similar to the American Hummer, but appeared to be much more durable. They were soon in the hills, and the cattle and the grass looked great. What a great adventure!

Then, over the next hill, a beautiful valley appeared. Baker and Walker were both amazed. It was as though everything had been painted with bright green paint. This was a short tour.

They went back to the ranch office, transferred to another vehicle, and returned to island headquarters with Upchurch and James. Upchurch told them he would like to be advised about the success of the plan for June the first. Baker took possession of the case containing the twenty-four vials of juice from the Rainbow Ball fruit and assured Upchurch that he would be notified about the results of the operation.

Baker and Walker went aboard a destroyer escort for the trip back to the aircraft carrier, then to Henderson field on Guadalcanal, and back to Washington. Both were quiet on the flight back to Washington, when finally Baker revealed to Walker that he had been having some thoughts he wanted to relay to him.

Baker said, "He was disturbed about the fact that this operation was going to kill twenty-four people. Over the years, there had been various execution methods in countries all around the world. But the people that actually performed the final act that caused the end of a life must have felt some guilt." He said, "I have been feeling some concern about what was going to happen on June the first." Baker continued, "After worrying about this, l came to the conclusion in order to bear the burden of guilt, l must be certain all of these intended victims were definitely guilty of crimes that are punishable by death. He had poured over the prepared list of twenty-four, and statements asserting that these people would have been on death row if it were not for some loop hole in the law that allowed them to wiggle free of punishment. After a lot of thought on this subject, I felt what we're doing is justified. Baker said, "He just wanted to relay my thoughts to Walker to see what his feelings were on these executions that are planned for June the first."

Walker agreed, "This could be a real problem for both of us. But the fact is it had been made clear from the beginning these deaths were innocent people who were, killed for greedy gain. Those who are responsible were tried, but, freed because of admissible evidence and technicalities." There was no more discussion about the matter.

Baker's mind felt a little more at ease.

SEVENTEEN

When they reached Washington, Baker was anxious to be relieved of the responsibility for the twenty-four vials of poison that he and Walker had brought back with them from the island of Bonita.

Albert O'Grady and Walt Carter, the two supervisors from Special Forces, were contacted by Baker and a meeting was set up so he could be dismissed of the vials of poison and final plans could be made.

They met at the same safe room where they could discuss matters without the fear of being over heard.

Baker asked about the progress of the agents assigned to Ed Leon in Los Angeles, Phillip Hatch of San Diego, Newt Aiken of Carson City, and Paul Shannon of Phoenix. The agents still had not been able to be in position to administer the poison on June the first.

O'Grady said "Since we have not been successful in the attempt to be able to get close enough to give them a dose of the poison, other plans are already in the making. Special marksmen have already been put into position to eliminate these four on June the first."

The plan would make it appear it was some group of organized crime was trying to eliminate the opposition. Hopefully, this would get some of the groups to eliminate others. The plan is that our agents will try to complete their task on the first or second of June.

Carter said, "It appears all of the other agents were in position to administer the poison to their selected subjects."

Baker told him, "Other agents are located in all of the selected cities, ready to get information published in the news about the deaths of the targeted four criminals. We need to get information out that rival gangs had killed the four. Although the other deaths would not show any cause of death, our agents would circulate information they had been suffocated or had choked on food."

Baker suggested that agents at each location be contacted and told to send Baker news items that referred to these deaths, but he planned to forward that information to Upchurch at Bonita Island.

Before leaving the meeting, Baker felt some relief as he passed the vials of poi-son to O'Grady and Carter. He left it up to them to determine who would be responsible for this very important liquid that had al-ready travelled about halfway around the world.

Carter took possession and said, "I'm going to make sure each of the agents are in a position to administer the needed dose and they would receive the poison in time to complete the plan on June the first." He will have four vials on hand since four of the twenty-four agents were unable to get in good position. He planned to place the vials in a secure safe. They could make plans at a later date to determine how to use these four remaining vials of poison.

Baker and Walker kept busy after they returned to the U.S. They were both in meetings for several days and the time passed by quickly. It was almost June 1st and both of them were getting nervous. Baker thought about the agents who were in position to administer the poison, and also, the four that were going to eliminate the four selected subjects. Agents that are assigned to this type of operation are never, under any condition mentioned in meetings or office memos by their names. Their names are never connected to the project to which they are being assigned. By doing this it is hoped that none of this information will ever be made public.

EIGHTEEN

June the first was a quiet day for Baker and Walker. They had made no appointments for this day and none for the second of June. The day started off, as usual, with coffee and donuts. They did not get any reports of the activities of the agents until four p.m. Washington time.

The report that Baker received was a memo from a TV special newscast from Carson City, Nevada. The report said that Newt Aiken had been shot dead as he was leaving his home this morning. Aiken lived in a very remote area that was secured by a fence and security guards. No other information was available at the time. But news-casters reported that Aiken was one of several persons that the D.A. has been trying to send to prison. It seemed that Aiken and his lawyers were sly enough so that the D.A. could never get enough information or evidence to present to the grand jury. It has been rumored that other groups were trying to take over the operation that Aiken was controlling. The D.A. commented that if his death, was gang-related there will probably be more deaths to come.

Baker was glad to receive information that the plan was starting to producing results. He and all his group of agents were very careful about any-thing being said or anything being placed on a memo. Nothing was ever said that could connect any of the group to any activity that was being referred to in any of this information.

Shortly after this first report of the plan, Baker received a message from Up-church stating that Price had made reservations to stay on the island for a week, beginning May 22nd. The reservation was confirmed by Price, and records indicated Price did arrive in Noumea on May 20th. However, there was no record of Price's location after May 22nd. It appeared he never arrived at Bonita. Baker knew what Upchurch was saying in that message. It had been determined that Price was the person that had been getting poison off the island, and there will be no more problems with Price as he had been eliminated. Everything was looking good for Baker and his group. It was getting late in the day and no additional reports had been received. Baker left for the day and was looking forward to tomorrow and receiving enough reports to confirm his plan that his had been successful.

What a surprise Baker had when he got to the office on the morning of June the second! Reports were coming in from everywhere it seemed. He counted eight reports. He was excited and hopeful for more reports as he started looking at what had been received.

The first report he read was a newscast that reported that Jeff Abel, who had mafia connections in the Newark, New Jersey, area, had suddenly collapsed while eating at one of his favorite restaurants. One of the reporters for the TV stations was present when this occurred, and he said emergency personnel were handling this as if he had already expired.

The next report was also from a TV newscast. This report said Ed Leon, known to have mafia connections, had been shot while entering an exercise gym. The report said Leon was known to work out at the gym about three times a week. Nothing more was said about his condition except that he was transported to Los Angeles hospital by an ambulance.

The next report said Harvey Steele was walking from a bank to his car outside a San Francisco bank when he collapsed on the sidewalk. The D.A. was in the process of trying to get Steele indicted by the grand jury because of his illegal activities. It appeared by the actions of the emergency personnel in attendance that Steele had died. Nothing was officially reported about his condition.

Baker was feeling good about the plan they had set up to get rid of a lot of undesirables and stop the flow of poison from the South Pacific to the group that were headed by Al Gotto. This action should stop the insurance killings.

The next report said Doug Felder was at the airport at Windsor Locks, Connecticut, waiting to meet someone coming in by private jet. Security later found him in his car. He was pronounced dead there. Nothing else was reported about this.

Edward Sorber was the subject of the next report. His housekeeper called 911 from his apartment in Manhattan, New York and reported he passed out while talking on the phone. He was listed as D.O.A. ("dead on arrival) by the emergency technicians. Newscast said he had lived in the area for about two years. Sorber came to Manhattan from Florida. He was known to be connected to the drug trade, both in Florida and Manhattan.

The next report was from Atlantic City, New Jersey. William Newby and an associate entered a cafe by the boardwalk and had just ordered the coffee when Newby seemed to have passed out. He was transported by ambulance to the local hospital. Nothing is known about his condition.

The next report was from the Bronx. Brian Wright, who lived in Manhattan, had just come out of an office building in the Bronx when he just passed out. This event took place several hours after the death of Edward Sorber in Manhattan. Even in the Big City, word gets around fast. It didn't take the police long to connect the two names. Nothing more was mentioned about his condition. It was assumed that 911 was called, but nothing else about his condition. Manhattan detectives had been working on drug cases, including both Wright and Sorber. This got their attention and they informed their boss about these two people. This was the last of the reports that were waiting for Baker when he arrived at his office on the second of June.

Other reports came in throughout the day. Baker had briefed Admiral Woodson, the Surgeon General of the U.S., about the project, and what was scheduled to happen on June first and second. Woodson and Baker had several conversations as to what information should be given to the news agencies. The best plan they could muster was this: there had been many deaths throughout the U.S. in the last two days. Many of the reported deaths were of people known to be involved in the distribution to sell drugs and other illegal operations. At this time we have not been able to determine the cause of these deaths. It is believed that some type of insect pesticide was sprayed in the fields where the drugs were being grown. All of the victims were known users of the drugs they were selling. As best we can tell, all of the drugs that these individuals had at the time of their death were transported into the U.S. by way of Mexico. We believe that many of the drugs came from the Pacific Coast and some of the countries south of Mexico.

The Surgeon General continued by issuing a warning against using any drugs that has entered this country from Mexico. He reminded everyone that it is not recommended to use any drugs from any location. In the case at hand, doing so could mean immediate death.

Baker and Woodson had worked on this speech for some time. There are also some state officials making statements along the same lines. Baker started reading other reports that were coming into the office. He thought how odd that Carl Woodson, an admiral in the Navy, would have the title of Surgeon General. Supposedly, they just pick the best person for that job, regardless of where they found them.

The first report he read after listening to Woodson's report was from Flagstaff, Arizona. Lance Hansen was reported to have been stricken while having breakfast at his home. The information was that his death was very sudden but, due to their law, he was not pronounced dead until transported to the local hospital.

The next report was the first failure. They had been unable to get an agent into position to administer the poison to Phillip Hatch in San Diego. Sharpshooters from Special Forces were brought in to eliminate him, but were unable to remove him from society by this method. The restrictions were to cancel the plan if unable to complete by noon on June the second. So this was a complete failure on that basis.

Roger Jacobs died as he was at the airport in Las Vegas. There was one reported death by gunfire that could be gang-related in New Jersey, where our agents had eliminated Jeff Able. There will probably be others.

There were also agents in place observing Al Gotto, who must be getting a little nervous. Our agents say that he has not been out of his house a since hearing about the first six or seven reports of death.

The five agents and I that had been helping at the border crossing between the U.S. and Mexico were back at the office in Irving. Admiral Baker thought it best we re-turn in the event of trouble with the plan that was being implemented.

On our flight back, we discussed what might be happening to the drug shipments that had escaped attention at the border crossings. We all thought the drug transporters might be changing their methods due to the statement by the Surgeon General about suspicion of drug contamination that might be causing immediate death. I suggested that eventually we should return to the border and follow a known load to its destination. We felt some of the shipments would be rejected and we wanted to see what would happen if that did occur. So after getting more reports of sudden death we contacted Baker and got an okay to go back to the southern border.

Baker was in his office early the next morning. Already he had several more reports. The first one was not related to this project but was a result of their plan. There had been a death by shooting in Manhattan. It was believed to be mafia-related. So it was as Baker had thought. As a result of these deaths, some of the drugs dealers would think other groups were responsible and would then retaliate.

The next report was from Hanford, Connecticut. Larry Perkins had a routine of jogging early every day. One morning, while jogging, he fell over dead. Friends said he was in excellent condition. Some even referred to him as a present-day Charles Atlas who in the late thirties had a body that was perfect and for a fee could help anyone have a perfect body too.

The next report was from New Brunswick, New Jersey. Morris Gento was well known by the local police. He was well connected to the local distribution of drugs but the D.A. could not get enough solid evidence to indict him. He was known to keep very late hours and always slept until after twelve noon. This night he was about to enter his home sometime after three in the morning. The local patrol observed him in a prone position on his front walkway. It was stated that he was pronounced D.O.A. at the local hospital.

Next a report came from Reno, Nevada. Al Carter was returning to Reno by car from his ranch, which was about twenty miles from Reno. The highway patrol found him in his car. There was no sign of foul play. It appeared that he just pulled off the road, crashed into a boulder, and died. No other information about him.

Paul Shannon was one of the twenty-four on our undesirable list. The report was that he had an argument with others at a local club in Phoenix, Arizona. He was shot and killed as he was leaving the club. The report did not list any suspects, but it indicated that drugs or drug money could be involved.

Baker had made an appointment to meet with Walker in Baker's office just before noon before heading to a small restaurant for lunch. Walker was excited to be meeting with Baker. He had been getting the same reports Baker had been receiving, but he was anxious to see what Baker had planned for the future.

They had a quiet lunch but did not discuss any of the current projects for fear of being overheard. The newsmen were always listening for any high-ranking official to unknowingly leak classified information. Baker and Walker knew they were being observed whenever they were in any public place.

For that reason, they did not discuss anything during their lunch that was not already public knowledge. Walker had a lot of questions for Baker. Just as soon as they got back to Baker's office, they both knew the office was a safe place to discuss anything. It was checked daily for listening devises.

Baker stated that reports were still coming into the office. Eleven had been successful and will likely have unknown causes of death. Three were removed by Special Forces sharpshooters. One was not removed because contact could not be made.

Baker said, "We are beginning to get reports that indicated the mafia must be thinking that the reported shootings were rival gang activity. It appears the mafia is starting to retaliate. We've had sixteen gunfire victims that we can tie in with this operation. Many more are expected."

Baker relayed his thoughts for the future, "By June 15th, all of the information we have obtained will be forward to Upchurch on Bonita Island by government courier. We will include a request to meet with him again in November. He will set the date and time of the meeting. The courier will wait for his reply. We will carry with us the complete results of this operation and will thank Upchurch for his help, and try to make sure we can do this same mission at least once a year and keep Upchurch informed so that he will know we are not using any of the poison for political purposes. He needs to know the poison will be used only on those escaping conviction in the courts."

NINETEEN

The other agents and I arrived at the Laredo border crossing between the U.S. and Mexico for a meeting with the U.S. officials at that area. We were curious as to what happened to the drugs at point of delivery. We speculated that most would be delivered as usual while some drugs would be rejected due to the drug scare brought on by the Surgeon General. Maybe one or two dealers would try to get a better price.

I explained to the officials that we wanted to identify a large shipment of drugs that was passing a checkpoint. Ideally, we would I.D. a car with hidden drugs and attach a G.T.D. to the car without alerting the driver or passengers. We wanted to do this so they could identify three cars. We would alert the D.P.S. officers in Temple, so they could monitor on their tracking device. This was agreed. We would all need to get a good night's sleep to be ready to follow subjects any time after 8 a.m. tomorrow.

Agents Jones and Small were assigned to the first suspects. The suspects were a couple appearing to be between forty and fifty years of age. The auto was a Ford four-door that was probably between six or seven years old, and looked as if it were well-cared-for. Border inspectors said a lot of drugs were hidden in the door panels, false trunk floor, and there was also one package under the hood. Agents were able to attach a G.T.D. without alerting the couple. They alerted D.P.S. at Temple, and Jones and Small headed north on Inter-state Highway 35, not far behind the couple who had the G.T.D. attached to their car. They kept the suspects a couple of miles ahead of them until they reached a point just north of Hillsboro. Interstate Highway 35 split at that point, the east section going to Dallas and the west part going to Fort Worth. This highway reconnects and continues north at Denton. The suspects took the east leg of Interstate 35, so the agents felt sure they would stop at the location where other carriers had been staying for an evening meal. The couple checked in at the same hotel others had used, then after a night's rest and breakfast they headed on to the north. As expected, the suspects stopped at the usual motel, located on the service road of Interstate 35. The location was next door to a restaurant.

With the G.T.D. device attached to the suspects' car, Agent Small knew they would be alerted by D.P.S. if subjects left before morning. With that assurance, Agent Small and Agent Jones relaxed a bit and located a restaurant and motel in a different location and would pick up surveillance tomorrow.

Agents Hope and Norris followed the next suspect with a tagged car. The suspect took Interstate 35 East into Dallas, but switched to Interstate 30 East and made no stops other than for gas until Greenville, Texas. The stop made was at a motel next to a restaurant and gas station. The agents felt the suspect would be there until morning, so they made arrangements for a room for the night, and for an evening meal. They stopped at another location so they would not come into contact with the suspects.

Watson and I tagged and followed the next suspects to their destination. These suspects proved to be a little different from the usual types who were smuggling drugs past the checkpoints at the border and on into the U.S. to a certain location. These suspects were two women travelling in a Volkswagen van that had been converted into a small motor home. The van had cabinets and seating that folded over to made a bed. Drugs were hidden in many places in the van. At the border crossing, everything appeared to be normal. The G.T.D. was attached to the van without attracting any attention. The two ladies left the checkpoint probably feeling that they had passed through without being detected. They continued north on Interstate 35 until reaching San Antonio. There they switched to Interstate 10 and it appeared that they were going to Houston. Late in the day they stopped at Seguin for an evening meal and a night's lodging. The way the women navigated the trip made it apparent that this was a repeat excursion.

We continued on Interstate 10 to the east for another forty-five miles before checking in for the night. We felt safe in doing this because there was no major city in that area and no interstate highway crossing close by. We would pick up the signal again first thing in the morning.

Baker was just about to read a new report about the sudden deaths when he received a message requesting his attendance for a 10:00am meeting in the Oval Office with the President of the United States the following morning. He put the reports down and decided it would be wise if he waited until after the meeting to learn of any more sudden-death victims. He felt the President knew what was happening. As always when they met, words had to be chosen very carefully. It was necessary the President know what was going on, but at the same time, it was very important that he be informed in a manner where he could truly say that he had not been told.

Baker was on time the next morning for the meeting with the President. He usually enjoyed these meetings. There was always a lot said without any firm statements or opinions. The President came into the room and had the usual greetings and small talk, and when the President spoke about the trip Baker and Walker had made to the

South Pacific, the President said the trip was long past due. He considered the visit with the governor of American Samoa to be one of the most needed contacts in the good-will tour. He said communications had been received from the Samoan government saying that it had been a long time since government officials had visited and he felt honored to have had visits from high-ranking officials. The President said comments had also been received from the officials in charge of the air field on Guadalcanal. He continued to talk about the trip with the President, commenting that he would like to see another goodwill trip to the general area in the next few months.

The President then asked Baker, "Have you heard the statement that the Surgeon General had made concerning the sudden deaths in various parts of the country?"

Baker replied, "I have heard the statement, and it seemed odd to me that reports were made about the deaths of only the ringleaders in the drugs trade. Surely, others had been affected as well." Baker continued, "It is assumed that some think these unknown causes of deaths are caused by organized crime gangs, and there have been several deaths by gunfire in retaliation to other gangs. If that were the case, it would be good if the gangs took care of each other, and eliminated some of the very evil ones that various district attorneys had been trying for years to place in jails so they can't do any more damage to society."

The meeting ended and Baker felt that he had conveyed to the President enough information about the sudden death of mafia-related persons. He also felt the President knew what was happening since he suggested Baker and Walker make another so-called good-will trip.

When Baker got back to his office, he immediately started reading the death re-ports that had been coming into his office. Lay Lawton in Harford, Connecticut, was a passenger in his chauffeur-driven auto when they were involved in a minor accident—nothing more than a couple of fairly good-dented fenders. After the confusion of the incident, the chauffer notified Lawton that they were ready to continue when he observed

Lawton was dead. This was confirmed by the emergency crew that arrived at the scene.

Las Vegas reports that Lewis Durrell passed out while at a dice table and was pronounced dead by both casino medical staff and city emergency personnel.

Reports from Darien, Connecticut show that Tony Bullock was found dead on a commuter train from Darien to New York City. It was very seldom that Bullock took the train into the city. No cause of death had been determined. They would wait for results from the autopsy.

Rudy Johnson from Yuma, Arizona, was returning home from the golf club late one afternoon and passed out just as he was getting out of his car in the family drive-way. The report does not indicate the cause of death but say that he was D.O.A. at hospital.

Another report came in from Niagara Falls, New York. Tony Horsley had some of the town guests at his home over the weekend. He and the guests had gone to see the falls. His wife reports any time they have visitors they always want to see the falls, so this trip was not out of the ordinary. This day Tony and the others were enjoying the view when Tony suddenly collapsed. Emergency services were summoned. One of the other sight-seers was an M.D. and he declared Tony to be dead at the scene. This was before other medical emergency teams arrived. Even though an M.D. had said he was dead, the state law required that subjects be transported to a local hospital and an official verdict be recorded about the condition. There had been no determination about the cause of death.

Larry Wilton was the subject of the next report from Phoenix, Arizona. This report said he was with a foursome that were just about to tee off for a round of golf when

Wilton was talking to the others and suddenly stopped talking and collapsed as though he had just fainted. It was later determined that he had died, with no cause of death indicated.

The report from Albany, New York, says that Mary Janik called 911 and reported she could not wake her husband, Eugene Janik, for breakfast. Emergency crews found him to be D.O.A. No more information could be provided.

Carrie Mosley of Newark, New Jersey, was the subject of the next report. He and his wife were celebrating their tenth wedding anniversary with a gathering of friends. They were just about to hear a short toast and drink champagne to celebrate the occasion when he passed out. There was no other information in the report except that 911 was called.

Los Angeles, California, reported that Ray Andrews was found at his desk as if he had been reading something on the desk and just went to sleep. His secretary had found him in that position and called 911 when she determined he could not be aroused. There was nothing more about this.

This last report of Andrews completed the results of the twenty four that had been planned by the group that had possession of the poison from the island of Bonita located in the South Pacific. A lot of the reports Baker received seem to indicate that the deaths resulted in gang retaliations, which was what Baker thought would happen. The results that his team accomplished with the poison caused these gangs to eliminate a great many of the opposing gang members.

TWENTY

Agents Jones and Small were elated when their subject started movement up the car at about nine the next morning. It appeared the couple was not in a hurry. They had been wise to stop for the night just before reaching Fort Worth. Fort Worth can be confusing navigating through, so it was good that they were going through this morning rather than after dark last night.

They made good time. They quickly passed through Denton and were still headed north on Interstate 35, stopping only once for gas and restroom. The couple must have grabbed ready-made sandwiches at the gas station, because they did not make a lunch stop. In Iowa, they switched over to Interstate Highway 80 and stopped for the night in Iowa City, still a good distance to Chicago, if that was their destination. They stayed the night in Iowa City and were back on the road by nine a.m., after breakfast and gas for the car. They changed to Interstate Highway 55 at Shorewood, Illinois. The agents both thought the couple would stay on 55 and switch to 57 and then 90 and come in on the south side of Chicago. They soon found out the reason they took that certain route. They stopped at Cicero, just a few miles from Chicago. It looked as if it was going to be the delivery location, so Agent Small notified the local police and gave them their location and asked for assistance, as a drug bust was about to take place.

The local drug enforcement group made contact with the agents just in time to see the Mexican suspects' car approached by two men in another car. After a few minutes, both cars drove two blocks and entered a warehouse by way of a drive-in door. The drug enforcement group soon had all four of the suspects in custody. The warehouse had been observed by local police for several months but they could not get an OK to make a raid on that location. This day was made easy because they were able to watch the suspects enter the building, and saw the beginnings of the drug deal go down. The agents headed back to Dallas and left the local police to clean up and make additional arrests.

Back in Texas, Agents Hope and Norris were following their suspects when they made a switch to Interstate 30 while in Dallas. The suspects were on the move now, traveling at the legal limit so as to not attract any attention or to be stopped for speeding. Soon they passed through Texarkana and continued into Arkansas on Interstate 30. Only one stop was made for food, gas, and other essentials.

There were a lot of signs along the way placed in obvious places that suggested a campaign to change the name of Benton, Arkansas. Some were suggesting that the new name should be Sam Walton. That made sense because he was the founder of the Wal-Mart stores. This became a very big company and probably most people in Benton worked for that company or the freight line that his brother-in-law owned. Other signs suggested changing the name to Wal-Mart. Others recommended that the name not be changed.

Agents Hope and Norris found a restaurant close to the location where the suspects had stopped. They would keep surveillance on them there. They were also tuned in on the G.T.D. that was placed on the suspects' car. The signal was picked up by D.P.S. at Temple, Texas. Their stop there was about one and a half hours, and they continued north on Interstate 30. At Little Rock, the suspects changed to Interstate 40, and they continued east on Interstate 40 across the Mississippi River and through Memphis. Still on Interstate 40, they made a stop at Bartlett, which was real close to Memphis. It appeared this would be their destination because the suspects seemed to know exactly where they were going.

They were in an industrial area that had many big warehouses. They parked outside of one of these warehouses. After observing them for about an hour, a car came alongside the suspects. All people from both cars met in the open and talked for thirty or forty minutes. Then they got back into their cars and left.

The agents followed the suspects towards a motel. They drove up, stayed a couple of minutes, and left. They repeated this at another motel. At the third, they checked in and went to their room. Agent Hope saw the room number that they had entered: room number thirty-one on the ground floor.

The suspects didn't stay in their room very long. They came out, got in the car, and drove a very short distance to the restaurant across the parking lot. This seemed very odd because it would have been much easier to just walk to the restaurant. There were vacant spaces on the parking lot near the door, but they parked near the back.

Then they entered the restaurant. Norris felt it was safe for him and Hope to have dinner at the same location. They had been very careful as they followed these two subjects and felt certain they had not been spotted. It was getting dark.

The agents had a seat in the restaurant where they could observe the subjects' car. They also had a view of room thirty-one. They had a good meal and were enjoying coffee when the suspects left the restaurant. The suspects went to their car and stayed there for a while. One of them opened the trunk as if looking for something and then closed the lid and both walked back toward the motel. Just before they reached room number thirty-one, the suspects' car exploded and was consumed by fire.

The suspects observed the fire and entered room thirty one. Agents Norris and Hope thought it was time to act. Hope called 911, explained to the operator that she and Norris were special agents that needed back-up at room thirty-one, and gave the location of the motel. Norris called the contact number in Memphis and gave the same information and asked for assistance from the drug enforcement officers.

After that, Norris and Hope prepared for action and headed for room thirty-one. Most of the occupants of rooms at the motel were in their doorway watching the fire. As the agents approached number thirty-one, they observed the suspects were also in their doorway watching the fire. The suspects were immediately taken into custody. The back-up they had asked for had arrived and shortly thereafter drug enforcement from Memphis arrived. The local fire department was at the scene of the car fire. With all of the extra help in the room, Norris explained to the suspects they had been observed from the time they had left Mexico. He told them it was known that they were transporting drugs when they entered the U.S. and the reason for their being followed was to see who was at the receiving end.

The suspects were definitely Mexican. One of them spoke very good English and indicated to Norris that he wanted to talk and would give them all of the information they needed. He wanted to have five people present for his exchange of information—his companion, Norris, Hope, one officer from Drug Enforcement in Memphis, and one local police officer. This was agreed and the others left the room.

This was a fair-sized room, but it was a lot better when the extras left. The suspect stated he wanted assurance that none of what he was going to say would be recorded. After that assurance, he began to talk, "My partner and I are both American citizens. Neither of us have a criminal record. What I am about to tell you is what I have heard has happened, really just hearsay and an assumption. Can I have your word that you will not use the information I tell you against me?"

All agreed and he started talking, "When we get through here, my friend and I will leave and will have no more contact with any of you. It is possible for an American to enter Mexico by auto, have drugs hidden in the car in Mexico, and come back to the U.S. You can take title to the car and also get I.D. papers under an assumed name so there is no record of you having been to Mexico at that time. I hope all of you understand that we are talking about what could have happened. If so, I shall continue. It has been assumed by the U.S. Surgeon General that a lot of deaths have occurred because of using drugs that have been harvested from an area that is using an unknown pesticide. This has affected the drug trade. Mexican drug lords feel that dealers in the U.S. will try to cut the price they pay for drugs. One drug lord has instructed his delivery people the action that they are to take if they are offered less than the agreed price. The drug costs the drug lord almost nothing. The main cost to him is in getting it to the dealer. His instructions to the delivery people was in the event that they are offered less, they are to burn the car with merchandise and contact the supplier, and the next shipment to the dealer will be at a higher price. I think we'll be leaving now."

This was okay with Agents Norris and Hope, and no one else objected.

Back in Washington, Baker was still getting reports of killing by gunfire of known gang members. This was not just happening in the city where poison had been administered, but in a lot of other larger cities. Gang members must be getting nervous. Al Gotto was staying at his home most of the time. He had plenty of his people on guard. Some of his gang members had been gunned down, but no attempt to get to him.

Baker was going to give all this information to Upchurch when they met again. He had not received a reply from Upchurch about a time and date for the meeting that he had requested in November.

Agent Watson and I had a good night's rest and breakfast at the coffee shop near the motel. We had continued on for about thirty-five miles after the suspects we were following had stopped for the night, and were waiting for suspects to start moving again. We knew that the tracking device would notify us when they started in the car. I had a feeling Houston would be the delivery point.

Traffic is usually very heavy during the day in Houston and Watson suggested we call our narcotic control contact in Houston and alert them so they wouldn't lose the suspects due to heavy traffic. When we made the call, we were informed that Houston had been making a very serious effort to control the drug trade and it was very likely the suspects would stop somewhere before they got to Houston. So the federal agents in Houston established a contact number for us, and said they would have agents located on Interstate 10, close to the western edge of Houston. They would be ready if the suspects did make a stop before entering the city.

The suspects must have had a good night in Seguin because it was almost 10 am before they started moving east on Interstate 10. We were aware when the suspects passed by our location, so we began to follow behind the suspects. The speed at which the suspects were travelling was much slower than the previous day. They kept a steady speed, and just after passing the Sam Houston Toll way, they exited onto Gessner Street.

When they exited, Watson immediately called the contact number for the Houston Narcotics Control Unit that was going to work with us. The unit advised Watson they would be in that area shortly, since they were now located on Interstate 10 just west of Loop 610. The suspects continued south on Gessner, they passed Buckner Hill Village, and stopped at a warehouse just before reaching Highway 59. The Houston unit met up with us and we all observed the suspects until they made contact outside one of the warehouses. The suspects talked with that contact for a few minutes, and then drove into one of the nearby warehouses. The Houston unit, along with us, closed in, captured the buyers, along with a lot of cash, and the Houston unit called for a special unit to search the van. This was a very clean drug bust. Lots of drugs were recovered along with a lot of cash. If appeared the buyer was not concerned that the drugs could be contaminated as suggested by the Surgeon General of the U.S. We left this in the hands of the Houston unit, and started back to Laredo.

Baker had received information from the courier that had been assigned to take a message to Upchurch on Bonita Island. Upchurch would expect Baker and Walker at 10 a.m. on November the fifth. Baker's schedule was clear for that day.

He was still getting reports of deaths from gang retaliations. Baker would have plenty of time to gather information on the activity this had caused in many cities in the U.S. Al Gotto was still alive but was not observed making many trips away from his home.

Baker contacted the Baker's Dozen. He instructed the six that were working with the Border Patrol to continue until after Baker had a meeting with Upchurch in November. The remaining seven of Baker's group were all working on similar problems that were scattered across the nation. We would meet as a group after the November meeting.

The Laredo group was enjoying our work with the Border Patrol. All had been trying to think of new ways to stop the drugs trade. Besides the drugs being smuggled past the checkpoints, much human-trafficking was taking place. The border guards determined that some of the people trying to get into the U.S. illegally had been given tranquillizers in order to keep them quiet until after leaving the checkpoint. This had made it more difficult to hear any noise coming from these people. Usually they were in the freight part of a freight trailer with cargo stacked between them and the rear of the trailer. Agent Jones came up with the idea of spraying pepper into the area of the trailer. Naturally, someone in the group had to ask the question, "Should we use red or black pepper?" Even doing this kind of work, it's good to have a little humor as you work on the problems. This really appeared to be a good idea. They got everything needed to spray the black pepper into the trailer and added a long piece of plastic pipe so as to reach deep into the trailer. After they got this ready for use, it was not long before they got an opportunity to see if it would produce results.

There was not any noise coming from the front part of the suspected trailer, but the border guard felt that it contained some illegals. We worked the pipe attachment to-wards the front of the trailer as best they could and started to spray the pepper. It did not take long to hear activity, sneezing, and coughing. After removing enough cargo to reach these people, ten exited from a very small area. Even though their trip to the U.S. was cut very short, they seemed to be very happy to be in fresh air.

The Border Patrol liked the idea and said it would be used at least twice a day.

Back in Washington, Baker was still getting reports on the gang killings. He felt they were the results of the gangs trying to get even with one another.

He had been called to meet with the President a few days earlier. The President told Baker that he was concerned about all of the corruption in Washington. Even though the room they were in was supposed to free from listening devices, they were careful about what they said.

The President said drugs coming into this country had been slowed and criminal gangs had been killing each other. Baker agreed he had received the same information. The President said since it was about time for Baker and Walker to make their good-will trip to the South Pacific, he was going to request that Baker use some of his time to help solve the problems in Washington. He requested that Baker instruct his group to determine what authority and what I.D. they would need to investigate any person on government payroll. This would include bank records, stock transactions, deeds to property, and title transfers. He told Baker that he wanted him to report back on the fifteenth of January.

TWENTY-ONE

Baker and Walker left for their trip to the South Pacific in plenty of time to meet with Upchurch on November the fifth at ten a.m. He and Walker had plans to really make this a good will tour and at the same time to meet with Upchurch on the island of Bonita.

The first stop on the tour would be Pearl Harbor. They met with the top officers at the naval base, did some public relation work with some local civilian officials, and tried to promote good will. They were there two days and moved on to Okinawa. The route they had chosen required extra traveling time, but was better than making a trip to each of these from the U.S. They did the usual two-day visit at Okinawa. One thing they noticed on Okinawa was that everything seemed to be fairly modern. I guess that would have to be true as almost everything on the island was destroyed in World War II. So not much there was over sixty years of age.

They moved on to Guam and had their usual two days there, and then to Port Moresby, New Guinea, and after their two days there they decided to skip Guadalcanal and go directly to Noumea, New Caledonia. This would allow an extra day of public relation work in Noumea before meeting with Upchurch on November the fifth at ten in the morning.

Everyone that Baker and Walker met with on this trip seemed to think it was really a good-will trip. They made the usual expected visits while in Noumea, had an evening meal, and retired for the night. Both were looking forward to the meeting with Upchurch the following morning.

They had received a message from the aircraft carrier that had been their transportation since leaving Pearl Harbor. That first leg of the trip was by air, with the remainder being by sea. The message they received requested that they allow a helicopter to pick them up at the landing pad at the hotel and join the aircraft carrier executive officer at breakfast before they arrived off the coast of Bonita for the 10:00 a.m. meeting. Baker and Walker agreed.

They arrived off the coast of Bonita with plenty of time to make the 10:00 a.m. meeting. They did the necessary radio contact and got permission to tie up at the dock at Bonita. The sea was calm. This was not unusual since stormy seas are a very unusual sight in this area. After docking the destroyer escort that transported them from the aircraft carrier to the island, they were taken directly to the reception area.

Upchurch was waiting for their arrival. They did the usual small talk, had coffee, talking about world events, and then Baker was ready to present the results of the plan to Upchurch. He had an individual report on each of the deaths. This included the known and also the suspected criminal activity on each person that had died as a result of this plan that involved the poison from the Rainbow Ball fruit. Baker gave the following report to Upchurch.

"The plan from the supplies that we received from you was to eliminate twenty-four very evil people. What we accomplished was this: twenty died from unknown cause; three were assassinated by our Special Forces; one was missed by the marksmen. Seventy-three were killed by other mafia members because they thought the other gang members had caused the deaths of the twenty three. The main person in need of being removed is Al Gotto. He has been staying very close to home and has a lot of guards. He

184 Calvin Kenneth Nix Sr.

will be removed after we return. Ninety-seven individual information sheets were presented to Upchurch. There was one sheet for each person involved."

They ended these talks and discussed the medical tests that were being conducted on the island, and then just had a very peaceful visit, which included a steak cookout at the ranch. It had been a good visit. Upchurch informed them that he had read the reports about the ninety seven involved in this plan. He was reassured that all deserved to die. He said that this operation could be repeated in the same manner on the fifteenth of April of each year, if that was agreeable to Baker and Walker, and if there were still many undesirables in the U.S. He agreed that supplies would be received well in advance and the plan would be put into effect on April the fifteenth. They had a good visit and Baker and Walker left the next morning.

The trip back to the U.S. was uneventful. They went back to Pearl Harbor by ship and from there to Washington by air. Baker notified the thirteen in his group to be in his office at ten a.m. on the eighth of December. This gave them several days to complete any unfinished business. Baker took advantage of this time to contact Special Forces and informed them to eliminate Al Gotto.

Two days later he received a memo that Al Gotto had been killed in an accident. He was leaving his home by car when the car was hit broadside by a very large construction truck. This was an accident. No charges were filled. Baker forwarded information to Upchurch on the island of Bonita, in the South Pacific.

When Baker's crew of thirteen arrived in his office on December the eighth, he gave them the results of the Bonita plan. Ninety-seven eliminated and the recent death of Al Gotto. Baker told them that all of them were due some time off. He said he had received a request from the President to come up with a workable plan to eliminate corruption that involved anyone being paid a salary by our government. This would include everyone (people employed for certain jobs, anyone elected to office, even including a dollar-a-year man) and in checking these, the trail probably will involve the lobbyists.

"While you're off for the holidays think of any special tools, permits, authorizations, or anything else that you will need." Baker told them that he felt that it would be a good idea to exempt from our project any elected officials who were in their first term. We will give them the benefit of the doubt. If they do a second term, then we will check all of their activities since being elected. Word will get out and maybe some of these newly-elected officials will stay clean.

With a slight grin, Baker told his crew, "Have a good holiday and I will see each of you back here, on January the third, at ten a.m."